MW01105397

The
RED
KETTLE

The RED KETTLE

Hidden in Plain Sight

JANELLE SCOTT

Order this book online at www.trafford.com
or email orders@trafford.com

Most Trafford titles are also available at major online book retailers.

Print information available on the last page.

ISBN: 978-1-4907-5988-3 (sc)
ISBN: 978-1-4907-5987-6 (hc)
ISBN: 978-1-4907-5986-9 (e)

Library of Congress Control Number: 2015907118

Because of the dynamic nature of the Internet, any web addresses or links contained in
this book may have changed since publication and may no longer be valid. The views
expressed in this work are solely those of the author and do not necessarily reflect the
views of the publisher, and the publisher hereby disclaims any responsibility for them.

Any people depicted in stock imagery provided by Thinkstock are models,
and such images are being used for illustrative purposes only.
Certain stock imagery © Thinkstock.

Trafford rev.   07/27/2015

 www.trafford.com

North America & international
toll-free: 1 888 232 4444 (USA & Canada)
fax: 812 355 4082

When I face my fears and conquer,
As a woman it makes me stronger.

Prologue

The scream of the sirens split the morning calm as the fire engines raced to the scene of a house where a large pile of rubbish was alight on the front lawn. A man was running around the edge of the fire and, as he threw pieces of clothing and what appeared to be toys, he was shouting "I told you I would give you nothing you bitch".

In the centre of the fire was a child's cot with the bedding well alight and sending sparks skywards. Scattered around the edges were the remains of what had already been burned and formed grey indistinguishable smouldering mounds of various sizes.

As the hoses were aimed at the heart of the fire it was not long before it was extinguished, but the man didn't seem to notice. He continued to throw female clothing onto the ashes, muttering to himself as he went back and forth to the house.

He was heard to say "You did what you were told before you got mixed up with that other woman. I hate her, I hate you and I am going to get rid of everything that you brought to this house. I am going to burn you out of existence and out of my memory".

The police had been called and as they tried to restrain him he raised his voice and yelled "Get away from me. It is all her fault and I am glad she has gone". This caused concern because nobody knew where the young woman was. She hadn't been seen since yesterday.

Chapter 1

T o say that Caroline was average would be kind. If you wanted to be honest you would describe her as forgettable. She was of average height, average weight, and average intelligence but had lovely turquoise eyes. Unfortunately her long fringe of mid-brown hair usually covered them up. Caroline used her fringe as a screen between her and the world.

Her mother was rather mousy in colouring, slightly on the short side in stature, and was neither fat nor thin. Her father was not the sort of person who would stand out in a crowd, even if there were only ten people making up that crowd.

Her parents' whole lives had been lived in the same suburb they grew up in and where they had both gone to school. They gravitated to each other in high school because they were usually the last ones standing when teams were chosen, exciting jobs given out or the other students being chosen for group sessions. Caroline followed in their footsteps.

They started going out together in high school, went to work in ordinary jobs, and then just stayed together. It wasn't as though either of them had to fight off suitors. They were well up in their twenties before they drifted into marriage. It was a happy time for them both, and they loved each other in a caring and supportive way, and each would do whatever was needed to make the other one happy.

He still worked in the local grocery store, where he had taken an afternoon job in high school and to everyone he was Stan—glad to climb a small step stool to take down a product from the top shelf, happy to keep the aisles free of the rubbish that seemed to accumulate throughout the day. It never occurred to him to try to better himself. He didn't aspire to own a racy sports car or keep climbing the property or social ladder. The only ladder Stan climbed was the one in the grocery store.

His wife Susannah, known as Sue, worked in the hairdressers. She looked after the ladies who liked perms and their hair set the same way every week. Sue wasn't one who would suggest changing the client's hair colour or style, so she had the same clients each week. She could be relied on to do a good job and was no challenge to the other stylists. By the time Sue was thirty-seven she had been working in the hairdressers for almost two decades. After being married for ten years she had long ago given up the idea that she and Stan would become a family, and it was a huge shock when she presented herself to the local GP, just not feeling up to par as she explained it, and after some questioning she was told, "You are pregnant."

She asked the doctor, "Are you sure?" and he just laughed.

"You will be a mum in six months," he announced.

Sue was waiting in the kitchen for Stan when he got home, and after the customary peck on his cheek she said, "You had better sit down, Stan, I have got something to tell you."

He looked a bit bewildered, and when she announced she was pregnant he just asked, "How?"

Sue just laughed at him and reminded him there was really no reason why she shouldn't be pregnant. After all, they had a very loving relationship, and he would be a dad in six months.

It was all a bit much for Stan, and he just flopped down into the nearest chair with a shocked look on his face. Wasn't Sue a bit old to be a first-time mother? That was his first thought and he hoped nothing would go wrong with the pregnancy or even more importantly his darling wife. Life wouldn't be worth living without her.

When Sue went to work the next day she told her boss she would have to leave in a few months because she was "expecting a little miracle." Her clients were all thrilled for her, and a lot of them set about knitting bonnets and booties for this "little miracle." The hairdresser's salon started to resemble a baby shop as more and more gifts were delivered to this delightful woman who had cut, permed, coloured, and set their hair for nearly twenty years. Sue hadn't expected any of this and was overwhelmed by her clients' generosity.

Sue and Stan started to prepare a nursery for their child. They were not great at home decoration but went out and bought paint and second-hand furniture, as they were not wealthy people, and he spent a lot of time out in the garage refurbishing all these treasures they had found and been given. Every so often, a neighbour or friend of a neighbour would turn up on their doorstep with "something for the baby." These gifts ranged from baskets of baby powder and creams to a beautiful pram that had hardly been used. The explanation for the excellent condition of the pram was that the parents hadn't known they were having twins, and two babies didn't fit in it for very long. It was very gratefully received.

It was an exciting time for them; Sue absolutely glowed throughout her pregnancy and had never looked prettier. She kept working up until she was about five months pregnant but then found that standing all day was just too tiring. She was happy to give up the full-time work at the salon but went in one day a week just to keep her hand in and earn a bit of money. It all helped to balance their meagre budget.

Sue's pregnancy was trouble free, and she was only three days away from her due date when she went into labour. She rang Stan at work, and he came screeching up the driveway in their little second-hand car to collect a very anxious Sue and drive her to the hospital. It was doubtful which one was the more nervous, Stan because of the impending birth or Sue because of Stan's erratic driving. She gently put a hand on his arm and begged him to slow down, as she wanted to get to hospital safely.

"I want to get to the hospital Maternity department not the Emergency department" Sue reminded Stan.

"Sorry darling, I am just a bit anxious to get you there on time".

Stan paced the corridor while Sue was admitted to the Maternity Unit. Hospitals were not encouraging of fathers being in the room when their child was born. Their job was to pace and wear out the linoleum in the waiting room until they were allowed to see the mother and child. It seemed like a long five hours to Stan, but he was too nervous to go and get a coffee or sandwich in case they came out looking for him.

A smiling nurse emerged from a room down the corridor and called out, "Is Mr Jensen here?" Stan couldn't speak from excitement so just raised his hand and was beckoned to come into the room. Sue was sitting up in bed with a big smile on her face, and there was a plastic crib just beside her with a white blanket wrapped around a sleeping bundle. Stan walked over and gave Sue a kiss and a hug and asked, "What have we got?" Sue replied, "A gorgeous little girl." They had picked out Caroline for a girl's name and both agreed that she looked like a "Caroline," whatever that meant. They couldn't have been happier and just kept looking at each other in wonder at this child they had created. Sue could hardly wait to get home and become a real mother to this wonderful little scrap of humanity. She had no trouble feeding her baby, and Stan was in awe of her competency in this whole new world they were now a part of—parenthood.

When Caroline was born, the most common comment was "what a nice little baby." She was neither bald nor had a good head of hair, of an average weight and length and rather pale in colouring. Those who knew her parents weren't really surprised that the girl was average, because both her parents could be described as just that.

Stan and Sue lived a very modest lifestyle, regularly paying their mortgage, and it would be a financial burden to have a second car when Caroline was due to go to school and later on to after-school activities. Stan would do anything for his beloved wife and daughter so asked for overtime at the store, but he then realised that most of the time he saw Caroline after work she was asleep and this didn't make him happy.

Sue had given up her hairdressing "career" to be a full-time mother and with the adjustment in their income Stan had to do an evening course in Small Business Management to increase his chances of promotion at the grocery store. He studied hard, even though he found it difficult, but he was doing it for his family and nothing was too good for them.

As most first-time parents know, babies do not read books on how to be a perfect child. They do not necessarily sleep the number of hours the books indicate, nor do they eat when they are supposed to of the quantities suggested. It is all trial and error on the part of the parents and sometimes they get it right and sometimes they don't. One thing is for sure—the new baby is running the show.

Caroline was an easy baby, contented and with a very ready smile. As she got older and started to pass all the milestones of sitting up, crawling, walking and then running, Sue and Stan were besotted with her. She had a sunny disposition, would amuse herself with her brightly coloured toys or was happy just watching the leaves move on the tree when she was put outside in her pram.

Everyone who met her as she went from baby to toddler to child commented on what a nice little girl she was. She was quiet and shy, as she didn't mix much with other children. Sue had rejected the idea of preschool as she wanted to enjoy her beloved daughter and it would be time enough to be separated when Caroline actually started school. Sue had already planned to go back to hairdressing part-time so she could fill in her days.

Caroline gave Sue and Stan many hours of joy as she progressed from sleeping in her cot to the bed that Stan had lovingly made for her. As Caroline got older Sundays were family day. The youngest member of the family could be safely left in the kitchen to get breakfast that was then delivered on a tray to her parent's bedroom.

"Are you ready for breakfast?" Sue and Stan would hear as Caroline appeared in the doorway, carefully balancing a tray decorated with a bunch of flowers picked from the garden that morning. They all piled into the one bed eating their way through cold toast and lukewarm coffee, but it was a special time for them all.

Sue enjoyed the days with her daughter as they baked irregular shaped cookies, made a special meal for Stan or just spent a few hours doing messy craft in the kitchen. The front of the fridge was soon full of the day's creations and Stan often had a hard time guessing exactly what Caroline had drawn or painted. Sue became adept at their own domestic sign language to try and give Stan a hint about the subject of the latest art work.

All too soon for Sue's liking, it was time for Caroline to start school. For weeks before the start of term there were uniforms to buy, school shoes to be fitted and endless questions to be answered.

"Will I find a friend Mum?" to which Sue always answered, "Of course you will darling".

"Will I like my teacher?" and Sue's reply was "Well, you will get to meet her a few days before you start school and she will show you where you will put your bag, and where you will be sitting in class. Maybe you will see a new friend then?".

However Sue was concerned that as Caroline was shy, she may feel left out for a while. This was mentioned to the teacher, out of Caroline's earshot, and Sue was reassured that Miss Briggs would be on the lookout for any problems. Sue went home feeling happy that her beloved daughter was being transferred to good hands for her school day.

School started for Caroline and each day she came home with another piece of almost dry painted paper with her name written in the top corner. More artwork for the front of the fridge but now both her parents had to guess what it was on the page. Not easy when you had not been privy to the instructions of what to paint.

As school progressed Caroline was a good student; attentive, punctual and always got a good report card. She was middle of the class with her grades but, to Sue's disappointment, she never seemed to make a special friend throughout her schooling. It didn't seem to concern Caroline all that much as she was used to being by herself. Eventually Sue stopped worrying about it because her daughter was obviously happy as she was.

Caroline was a plain child and if a tree was needed in a school play, she got the part. She was quiet, obedient, and even as a hormonally charged teenager she abided by the family rules. She wasn't behind the toilet block after school smoking stolen cigarettes, as were the "popular" girls. Caroline was at the bus stop to catch her regular bus home. Her classmates made fun of her and called her all sorts of derogatory names, but by the time she got to be a teenager she was immune to this type of treatment. It had gone on all her life.

When she reached home her mother had some food and a drink waiting for her and liked to hear about her day at school. This conversation didn't last long because for Caroline each day was much like any other. She didn't have any special friend and spent most of her lunchtimes by herself, under the shade of a tree in the schoolyard. She didn't get chosen for a solo in the choir or the lead in a dancing concert so there wasn't much to tell.

She didn't go to school dances because she had no one to go with, but it didn't really worry her. She was an only child, but she was well loved by both her parents and felt safe and secure at home. She wasn't expected to help with the housework, washing, ironing, or cooking, as that was her mother's domain.

With the added responsibilities of a promotion her father had taken on at work to balance the budget, he didn't get home until seven most nights so Caroline didn't see much of him but he was always available for a chat after he had his dinner and she looked forward to this time with her father.

She shied away from sports, mainly because she wasn't any good at any of them and was an absolute klutz with any game involving a ball. She wasn't even considered good enough to be the last reserve for anything, so spent a lot of time in the library reading about other people's lives.

She wasn't unhappy, but she was lonely. The girls who had been reasonably friendly to her were pairing up with boyfriends and didn't want Caroline along to make up a threesome. Her limited social life dried up and she spent more and more time at home in her room, listening to music and reading books. There was no spare money in the household to spend on glossy fashion magazines so her sense of the latest trends was sadly lacking. She wasn't really interested in how she looked, and no matter what she wore; nobody made any comment, complimentary or otherwise.

Due to a lack of activity Caroline started to put on weight and was miserable about it. Although she had never been interested in fashion she realised that not only was she out of step with the latest "cool gear" but that what clothing she did have was getting tighter and tighter, and not in a flattering way. Her mother could see that her daughter was ballooning, not blossoming, and after talking it over with Stan, they decided to get her a dog so she could get some exercise and perhaps lose some weight. Well, that was the plan.

In their inexperience, but with good intentions, they brought home a retired greyhound called Hurricane, or Hurry for short. Their thought process was that a greyhound would need daily exercise. However, they hadn't counted on the fact that the reason this greyhound was retired was because he was bone-lazy. Whoever had named it Hurricane had obviously never seen him run—which was reasonable, because he didn't. Hurry just took up most of the lounge and could be found there at any time of the day or night.

Caroline quickly learned that the only time Hurry actually hurried was when she took his lead from behind the laundry door, which signalled that they were going for a walk, and he disappeared at a spanking pace right up to the end of the backyard and under a prickly bush so she couldn't grab him. He had managed to dig himself a hole deep enough so that the prickly branches didn't catch him, but they would certainly scratch anyone keen enough to try to put a lead on him.

When he thought the coast was clear, or it was too dark to go for a walk, he would saunter back to the house, climb through the doggy door, and take up his position on the lounge. Life was pretty good for Hurry and he had no plans to change it.

In the absence of Hurry accompanying Caroline on a walk, she decided that the one thing she liked to do was swim. She didn't need a partner for it, which was a bonus, she could do it in any weather and it would get her weight down. The one obstacle to this was that she hated how she looked in a swimming costume. Sue was very encouraging of this swimming idea and offered to drive her daughter to and from the pool and swim the lanes with her. Caroline was very grateful for her mother's support and set off to find a swimming costume that was as flattering as possible.

After trying on most of the ones available in her size at the local boutique, she said to Sue "Mum I hate how I look in any of them. How am I going to go out in public looking like a floral whale?" Sue had a hard time not laughing as she tried to imagine what a flower bedecked whale would actually look like. It was not the time to show any sign of humour as her daughter was obviously distressed by what the mirror reflected back at her.

Sue decided to try another approach. "Why don't we go and have a nice lunch, then have a look in some of the department stores. Maybe you will see something there that you like?" Caroline reluctantly agreed and with slumped shoulders she flopped into a chair at the nearest coffee shop and looked miserable.

"You know Caroline, the whole purpose of buying this swimming costume is to swim. If it will make you feel better, why not wear a great looking T-shirt over it when you get out of the pool?" Caroline just raised one eyebrow to indicate that this was a really dumb idea. She would still look fat, but wearing a T-shirt to cover up.

After lunch they went to the swimwear section of the nearest department store where the range was much larger than in the boutique stores they had already visited. Caroline walked disconsolately along the racks until she found something she thought would be okay and took it into the change room.

"Mum, come and have a look at this and tell me what you think?" came a voice from behind the curtain. Caroline pulled the curtain aside and Sue was pleased at how her daughter looked. "You look lovely. I think that is the one for you, but I also have a suggestion. How about you try on some more and choose another in a smaller size that you really love and can wear when she get your weight down?" Incentive was the name of the game.

Caroline returned to the racks and after careful inspection of smaller sizes, found one that she felt would be flattering and took it back into the change room. She emerged 10 minutes later with a beaming smile. Mission accomplished.

Sue was becoming concerned about her daughter's chances of finding a life partner. Caroline didn't have a social life; girls in her class were rocketing from one relationship to another but she herself had never had a date and she was eighteen next birthday. It was pointless planning a party; there was no one to invite. The phone was silent; nobody rang to invite Caroline out, even to the movies.

Sue was sad for her daughter and thought it would be a good idea to send Caroline on a holiday where she might meet some young people. Caroline greeted this news with absolute horror and pleaded with her mother to get her money back. She just didn't fit in anywhere and had spent years being the one left out, therefore growing up to be painfully shy. "Sending me for two weeks to be amongst strangers would be worse than having all my teeth pulled out, without anaesthetic," Caroline explained.

In her last year of high school, invitations to parties were being sent by electronic means either on phones, iPad, emails or Facebook but Caroline didn't have access to any of these. What would be the point—there was no one whom she cared to contact and she certainly wouldn't be sitting around checking for emails that never came.

The school was having a formal for those leaving in year 12, but Caroline did not have the desire or the courage to go. The girls were twittering on about what colour their dresses were going to be, the style, their shoes, how they were going to have their hair done, what sort of limo was picking them up, and last but not least, whom they were going with. Not one person asked any of these questions of Caroline. They assumed, correctly, that she was not going to be there.

On the last day of school, she went quietly to her locker, took out her spare jacket and other personal bits and pieces, and walked out the school gates for the last time. Nobody saw her leave and even if they did, it is doubtful whether they would have cared.

Caroline's school results were average, as expected, and she got a job as a junior secretary with a city-based company. She was always on time to start work, dressed neatly and was well groomed. However, if a colleague were directed to "give this to Caroline" inevitably he or she would reply, "Who?"

On one particularly bitterly cold day, she was carrying her take-away coffee towards work, and had her head down to stop her hair blowing across her face. She slammed into a body coming the other way and deposited hot latte all down the front of his crisp white shirt and brown suit. She was horrified, he was angry and was now drenched in coffee.

Caroline, trying to be helpful, pulled her new red scarf from around her neck and tried to mop up the coffee from his shirt, but all she succeeded in doing was to make the caramel colour go a peculiar shade of pink.

"I am so sorry. I didn't see you" Caroline stammered.

The young man she had collided with roughly pushed her away and said, "Next time, look where you are going" and rushed towards a set of lifts, the doors of which were in the process of closing. He disappeared into the narrowing gap and Caroline hoped she would never see him again.

She knew that if she didn't hurry she would be late for work and that would never do. She prided herself on always being on time, but this morning's debacle had used up precious minutes. As she was on her way down the corridor to her cupboard they called an office, she heard a man's voice saying, "Sorry I am a mess, but some stupid female with a coffee in her hand almost knocked me down and threw her coffee all over me." That voice had a familiar ring about it and when Caroline poked her nose out the door of her office, she could see the back of a brown suit and the collar of a white shirt, topped off by windblown brown hair. *Oh no, not him.*

The new junior accountant had arrived and would be working in the same office as Caroline. Some days are just for staying in bed.

Chapter 2

Caroline had continued her swimming program over the years and both she and Sue had lost weight and had very trim figures, but they both would have been very embarrassed if this fact had been mentioned by anyone outside the house. Caroline dressed neatly and rather conservatively for her work days and still didn't realise how lovely she looked. She spent very little time looking in a mirror. Her hair was shoulder length and only needed a good brush to have it shining and framing her face. Her skin was a perfect cream and housed her beautiful eyes and long silky lashes.

She moaned to her mother when she was younger that she was an ugly duckling and her mother just laughed. "You are certainly nothing like an ugly duckling, but if you persist with that description of yourself, just think what happened to that particular bird. She grew into a graceful swan didn't she?" Caroline nodded, but was not convinced that was her future.

Caroline continued on in her less than challenging role as a junior secretary for many years, and like her parents before her, didn't seek to climb the corporate ladder. She was quite content with her role and her pay packet and, without the confidence to apply for a new position; she was destined to stay on the lower rungs. She hadn't made any friends but would sometimes join the crowd for Friday night drinks when the general call went out, "Everybody to the pub tonight," and just to ease the loneliness and boredom she would occasionally go.

If a survey were taken of how often Caroline went to the pub on Friday night, or which Friday night, it is doubtful that anyone would remember with any great degree of accuracy. She just blended in to the background and the only person who seemed to take any notice of her on those occasions was Owen, the junior accountant, on whom she had emptied her coffee cup the first day he worked for the company.

Owen didn't fit in with this young group of people either. He had a very inflated opinion of himself and his abilities, which didn't endear him to his male colleagues, and the girls thought he was a nerd. He, like Caroline, was average. He was of average height, weight, and colouring and really had nothing to recommend him to any female. He strutted around the office as though "he had a broom up his arse," as one of his colleagues commented.

His desk had an IN tray on the right and an OUT tray on the left. Between these two trays was one container with six sharpened pencils and four pens—one black, one blue, one red, and one green. Sometimes when Owen went out on his one-hour lunch break, taking his home-made lunch in a paper bag, a colleague would go into his office and do something they knew would annoy him.

On one occasion they replaced the sharpened pencils with blunt ones that had been chewed at the other end. Owen always reacted in the same way. On that occasion, he picked up all the pencils and threw them in the nearest bin outside his office, went to the stationery cupboard and chose another six pencils, made a show of sharpening them, and replaced them in his container. Another of their tricks was to mix up the contents of the IN tray and OUT tray correspondence. It then took Owen the rest of the afternoon to re-sort it. It didn't amuse him, but it took the boredom factor out of other people's days.

In the office Owen and Caroline were polite to each other, but on those occasional Friday pub nights, they stood or sat together for the simple reason that nobody else sought out their company, as they weren't interested in what they had to say. On one occasion Owen surprised Caroline by asking her "Are you going to the pub tonight". It took her a moment to answer, "Yes, I suppose so. I don't have anything else to do".

Owen was a few years older than Caroline and seemed so worldly to her. He too had led a sheltered life, his mother being widowed when Owen was quite young. Most of his "worldliness" was acquired from reading books about other people's lives and watching documentaries on television in his bedroom after his mother had gone to bed. He made sure that she never saw the "stud" magazines he occasionally bought and would secrete them inside a book he was supposedly reading.

When he had first started with the company he had asked one or two of the girls out and was a bit mystified by their response of "No, I can't." Their excuses ranged from "I have to pluck my eyebrows tonight" or "wash my hair" to "I have to sit with my sick dog." At no time did Owen realise that they actually didn't want to go out with him. He was so arrogant and thought that they were missing out on a great opportunity to share time with a well-educated and intelligent man, and it was their loss, not his. He had never travelled further than the nearest capital city, about twenty-five kilometres away, and thought "So what?"

Owen was lacking in personality, to say the least, and always wore brown suits in various shades with brown shoes. All his shirts were white, and he had five ties in muted tones of brown and cream—one for each day of the week. It was even possible that he had an allocated Monday tie, Tuesday tie, etc., but nobody was interested enough to keep a check. He always looked the same to most people, if they even bothered to think about it.

Caroline and Owen's weekend social life was very similar—empty of any places to be, people to be with, or a time they needed to arrive anywhere. On Monday morning while gathered around the water cooler, the other office staff would exchange stories of their weekend, some in far too much graphic detail for either Caroline or Owen to feel comfortable with. There were stories of after footie punch-ups, drunken pub crawls (and that was by the girls)—and there was no information left out on their sexual couplings either.

It was at the point of the sexual exploits and lovemaking positions that Owen and Caroline would quietly leave, with their cups of water, and go to their separate desks with a rather pink glow to their cheeks.

Neither of them had done anything on their weekend to compete with the stories by their colleagues.

After one of the girls gave a very descriptive version of her latest one-night stand, Owen remarked to Caroline "What a tart. It is a well known fact that females don't enjoy sex as much as a man" and with that comment he disappeared around the corner. Caroline was left standing in the corridor with a bemused expression on her face. *What would he know? He had never had a girlfriend as far as I know.*

Caroline was twenty-five years old, still a virgin, and had only been out with a few men. One of them had been a sales rep, Paul, who called into the office to see her as she showed him through to her boss's office. He had been rather taken with Caroline's quiet demeanour and gorgeous eyes. He checked with her boss that she wasn't married on in a relationship before he asked her "Would you like to go out for dinner one night with me?" Caroline was taken quite by surprise and only barely managed to stammer out her reply of "Ah, no I don't think so, but thank you anyway".

Not to be put off, when he next came into the office he tried again. "I really would like to take you out to dinner Caroline. What night would suit you?" Faced with such a definite invitation she agreed to Saturday night. "I will pick you up at about 7 pm if that is okay. What type of food do you like to eat" and Caroline managed to reply "Well, anything really, but I don't like food that is too spicy".

After giving him her address, she fled back to her office cupboard with her cheeks glowing. He seemed very nice, polite, well dressed and it would be a change to go out to dinner with just one other person instead of pizzas with the work crowd on Friday night.

Promptly at 7 p.m. Saturday night Paul knocked on the door of Caroline's home. From his position on the lounge Hurry raised his head and gave out one of his "there is someone at the door" barks, but it didn't seem important enough for him to move. Caroline gave him a pat as she went past her best friend and opened the front door. Paul stood there with a lovely bunch of flowers for her that didn't look like they had come from the buckets at the local service station.

"Thank you. They are really beautiful," she said. "Just like you" Paul replied.

"Would you like to come in and meet mum and dad?" Caroline politely enquired as Paul stepped into the hallway.

"Good evening," Paul greeted her mother and shook hands with her father.

There was a bit of small talk followed by "Have a lovely evening you two" said Sue as she handed Caroline her coat.

"We will," they chorused.

"I have booked us a table for 7.30 at the Dolca Vita, so we will have time for a drink first if you would like" Paul told Caroline and she replied "That would be lovely. Thank you". *What a gentleman, and so thoughtful. Oh well, here goes.*

After a lovely dinner, and just before dessert, Paul mentioned that he was married, but he emphasised the point that he was separated. Caroline was shocked as she hadn't expected this revelation. "How long have you been separated?" she managed to ask. "Only 3 months but we won't be getting back together" Paul answered. "We are living separate lives, but are still in the same house. For convenience" he added in reply to Caroline's raised eyebrows and sceptical look.

Coffee was followed by Caroline's request to be taken home. "I thought we might go somewhere and look at the moon over the water" was Paul's reply.

"No thanks, I just want to go home, and for the record I don't date married men". *Or any men for that matter, but when someone asks me out in the future I will be checking their marital status.*

An awkward silence followed and with a shrug of his shoulders Paul agreed to take Caroline home. He pulled the car up out the front of her house, leaned across her and opened the door. Caroline noted that her exit from the car was very different to when they were leaving her home. He had opened the door, from the outside, and seen her settled comfortably in the seat. "I am separated you know" he once again mentioned from where he was sitting behind the wheel of the car, obviously with no intention of going around to help her out.

"I don't care if you are separated. You are not free to embark on another relationship and I am upset you weren't upfront with me about it"

"If I had been honest I know you wouldn't have gone out with me." Paul thought he had had the last word when Caroline came back with "You are absolutely right on that score. Good night." *And don't think I am going to thank you for being dishonest with me. That is a trait I can't stand.*

Caroline wasn't even to her front door before Paul slammed the car into gear and roared up the road, obviously in quite a temper. When she got inside, Sue popped her head out from the bedroom and said, "How did it go? I heard a car leave in a squeal of tyres."

"I will tell you all about it in the morning Mum" as Caroline gave her mother a goodnight kiss on the cheek.

Sue was amazed that such a polite young man had been such a disappointment and felt sad for her daughter. Once again Sue realised how lucky she had been to find Stan and not have to go through what Caroline was experiencing.

Caroline continued to go out now and again, but didn't have much luck with men. She was inexperienced in the dating world and was not about to repeat the exploits of the girls in the office as they recounted their weekend activities.

She didn't realise how attractive she was. She was always surprised when a male spoke to her, even if it was the new butcher in the neighbourhood or the guy in the bottle shop who was doing the afternoon shift. Caroline usually made her purchase and bolted out the door as soon as she had received her change.

On one occasion in the supermarket the assistant manager, who looked to be about Caroline's age, asked her if he could be of any assistance as she wandered the aisles looking for a particular cake ingredient for Sue. He told her his name was Garry "Just follow me and I will show you where it is" as Caroline followed him down a long aisle.

"I have seen you in here a few times, but I wasn't brave enough to speak to you" he informed Caroline. "I have been wanting to ask you out but I don't know your name. Would you go out with me?"

"Before I tell you my name or anything about me, I would just like to ask you a question."

"Sure, go ahead. Anything you want." Caroline surprised him with her question "Are you married, engaged or in a relationship?"

"None of the above and never have been. I have been too busy doing my Business Management Course to go on dates for the last few years. So, now will you go out with me?"

"Okay, but just for a coffee or a drink after work if that is okay with you".

"Sure, anything you would like to do is fine with me. I finish work at 7 tonight, so would that be okay if you are free?"

They made arrangements to meet at a local wine bar that had recently opened.

Caroline and Garry talked for a while, but found that they didn't have much in common and there was no real chemistry. After two drinks they said goodbye and made their separate ways home.

A few of the girls at work wanted her to go out with someone to make up a foursome when it suited them but she was reluctant because of the tales around the water cooler. She was nervous about going on blind dates, but occasionally agreed so that they would leave her alone. Most of the females she worked with could not comprehend that this gorgeous girl did not have a permanent man in her life. They certainly didn't count Owen as a contender. In fact, they didn't actually count Owen in any way at all.

Caroline tried going out with a few men but none of them asked her out again, and she wasn't confident enough to suggest a second date to them. She was pleasant company, but by no means a sparkling conversationalist, although the men she went out with over the years were quite happy to talk about themselves anyway. She just needed to nod in the right places.

At the end of the evening, sometimes they took her home and other times they didn't and she became used to getting a taxi. It was worth the fare to know she would get home and avoid the awkwardness of deciding whether to invite them in for coffee or not. On one occasion she had allowed her date to drive her home and there had been quite a scuffle on her doorstep. He had been somewhat determined that his evening was unfinished and drinking coffee was not his first choice for the finale. Caroline had become adept at putting her key in the lock very quickly and shutting the front door just as fast, leaving her latest date on the doorstep with a surprised look on his face.

It was not necessary for Caroline to keep a pen and paper in her bag to give them her phone number, because none of them ever asked for it. She was not really attracted to any of them, but went out just for something to do. She admitted to herself that she was lonely, but at least she was alone on her own terms.

Chapter 3

Owen was taken to hospital with appendicitis and the office voted Caroline to go and see him, mainly because none of the others could be bothered to use up their precious hours visiting a patient whom they rarely spoke to even in the office. A bunch of flowers and a box of chocolates, of an inferior quality so as to not waste money from the fund set aside for such purposes, were duly purchased and the florist's small square of white cardboard that was attached had the greeting "Get Well Soon from your workmates." It was agreed that it wasn't worth the effort of getting a big card for all the staff to sign. Most would ask, "Owen who?"

Caroline was quietly chuffed about being asked to deliver the flowers and chocolates to Owen and was unaware of the sentiments behind her mission. She caught two buses to the hospital, had a quick bite to eat in the canteen available for visitors, and duly presented herself to Ward 2E right at the start of visiting hours. Caroline was never late for anything, even hospital visiting hours.

She made her way down the middle of the room to the last bed on the left. He was sitting up in bed in brown-and-white-striped pyjamas, reading the daily paper finance section. To say he was surprised to see her was an understatement and it took a moment or two for him to regain his composure.

Quietly she said "Hi Owen, how are you feeling?"

With a surprised look on his face, he asked pleasantly, "What are you doing here?" as she emerged from behind the bunch of flowers and attempted to put the chocolates on top of the miniscule locker before they could drop to the floor. She was quite breathless with all this activity and sat down on the chair beside his bed. She blushed at seeing him in pyjamas; the only other male she had seen in this state of undress was her father. She explained that she had been asked to bring the flowers and chocolates to him on behalf of the rest of the staff and extend their good wishes for his speedy recovery, all of which Owen accepted with a wry smile. He knew he wouldn't win any popularity contests at work, but that was the story of his life. The opinion of his work colleagues was of no interest to Owen.

They exchanged pleasantries about what was happening at work, in the big world, and about Owen's expected date of release. He only lived a few kilometres from Caroline so she offered to borrow her father's car and pick him up when he was discharged on the weekend and drive him home. "That's very kind of you, Caroline. Thank you," he replied.

On Saturday morning, she put his plastic bag of belongings on the back seat and settled him in the front. "Are you comfortable?" Caroline asked him. She was very shy in his company but was glad to do this good deed for someone who had just come out of hospital. At his place, she carried the plastic bag, helped him up the few front steps and inside the house. His mother had died two years ago and left the house to him as he was an only child. It was in need of a bit of maintenance and looked as though it had been untouched for years, but Owen wasn't much of a handyman and preferred not to spend any money on it that wasn't absolutely necessary.

"Thanks Caroline. That was very kind of you. I would have struggled getting public transport home."

"You could have caught a taxi" Caroline commented and Owen just looked at her and shook his head. "I am not wasting my hard earned money on taxis, thanks very much."

"I can at least offer you a cup of tea or coffee if you would like." Caroline agreed that would be nice so Owen put the kettle on the old-fashioned stove and lit the gas. He took down two sets of Royal Albert cups and saucers, beautifully decorated with roses, and a sugar basin to match. Very plain biscuits appeared from the further depths of the cupboard and were placed in neat rows on a china plate from the same set. The tea was made from leaves, not a tea bag that Owen said he considered pure waste, and at last they were ready to sit down.

Caroline started off with "What was your childhood like Owen?"

"Well, I am an only child and my mother told me that I was quite a surprise, arriving as I did so late in my parent's life".

"Did you have any pets to keep you company?" Caroline asked.

"Yes, I had a rabbit but when he died I wasn't allowed to have any more pets. My mother said they made too much mess".

"What about you Caroline? Any pets in your childhood?"

"Yes, I still have my lazy greyhound Hurry and I love him to bits".

Owen looked rather surprised that someone expressed so much emotion over a pet, but when he looked back at how he felt when Bunny dug under the fence and escaped, he understood.

After an hour or so the conversation started to run out of steam, so Caroline said her goodbyes, Owen thanked her for picking him up from the hospital and rather tentatively placed a chaste kiss on her cheek. She blushed bright pink and almost fell down the steps in her haste to get into the car. She didn't need to worry about waving goodbye as Owen had already shut the front door. If he let the cold air in he would have to turn up the heat, and that would be a waste of money.

On the way home her father's car cut out a few times for no apparent reason. There was enough fuel according to the gauge, and the temperature was in the middle as it should be, but Caroline mentioned it to her father when she got home.

"Dad, the car cut out a few times on me today but all the gauges seemed okay."

"I will get it checked out tomorrow. It might just be a fuel blockage or something like that. Probably nothing too serious as you got home okay."

He said that he and her mother were going to the movies, but he would get it checked the next day. At seven, Caroline waved her parents off, made a hot drink, watched a chick flick on television and turned out the lights at eleven-thirty. Hurry curled himself up on the bottom of the bed and they both slept soundly until awakened by a loud banging on the front door. She was a bit confused as her parents had keys, unless they had lost them, and when she had a look through the security screen there were two police men standing there.

Their opening question was "Is this the home of Mr and Mrs Jensen?"

The more senior of the two said, "May we come in, we have some bad news I am sorry to say." Caroline almost collapsed at the doorway but managed to open the screen door and ushered them into the lounge area.

The police explained that her parents' car had stopped suddenly in the middle of an intersection and was hit from behind by a truck. The truck driver said that there had been no brake lights. Caroline remembered the way the car had been cutting out the night before when she was driving. Perhaps the fault had occurred again. The police tried to reassure Caroline that her parents would not have suffered as they were killed instantly, but it was little comfort.

"Is there anyone we can ring for you?" the younger policeman enquired and Caroline just shook her head. She couldn't answer them but they offered to get a neighbour to stay with her. She was numb and when she lifted her head, the tears continued to run down her cheeks and drip off her chin. Her kindly neighbour, Wendy, came in as soon as the police asked her to, and Caroline sobbed into her shoulder. She had known Caroline all her life and felt so sorry for her loss because she was now on her own in the world.

Caroline declined Wendy's kind offer to stay at her place, as she didn't want to leave Hurry alone. In his doggy way he knew there was something wrong in his beloved owner's world. Caroline couldn't sleep but tossed and turned until the early hours of the morning. There was just her and Hurry now and, he left his position on the lounge, a rare thing indeed as he was thirteen years old now. He tried to climb up with Caroline but his poor old arthritic legs wouldn't let him. He let his greying muzzle rest gently in her lap and her hands stroked his dear old faithful head while her tears dripped down onto him.

The only two people who mattered to her in the world weren't coming home ever again. *What on earth am I going to do now?*

Chapter 4

The morning after her parents' deaths the only person Caroline could think to call was Owen. She was alone in the world and, as he had lost his mother two years earlier, she thought he would understand.

When Owen eventually answered the phone, he was slightly out of breath. "Are you okay?" enquired Caroline, being concerned for him.

"Why, who is this?" Owen snapped.

"It's Caroline. I just wanted to let you know that my parents were killed in an accident last night and I don't know what to do" she explained to him, in a rather teary voice.

"Oh Caroline, that's awful. Do you want me to come over?"

He went on to explain he didn't have a car, as he considered them a waste of money. It would take him too long to come over in the bus, but he asked her if there was anything he could do for her under the circumstances.

"No, it's alright. I just wanted someone to talk to. Wendy from next door will help me so I will go and see her. I will be okay. Bye."

There was no way that Owen was going to get a taxi to go over and comfort this girl who just worked in his office, though she was nice enough, he supposed. After all, she had picked him up from the hospital and taken him home, but he wasn't prepared to put himself out that much, and on a Sunday too.

Owen went back to reading the weekend papers and didn't give Caroline's dilemma another thought. He went to work the next morning and received a few cursory enquiries as to his health after his appendectomy. Not being one to miss an opportunity to be the centre of attention, as his work colleagues usually ignored him, he then launched into telling anyone who would listen about the tragedy that had befallen Caroline. There were the usual "how awful" and "it must be dreadful for her" but beyond that nobody thought to call her to see how she was faring. They just didn't know her that well and were totally unaware of her family structure. Some concluded that she had relatives who would rally around and help her through this.

Later in the day Caroline's boss contacted her, and Caroline tearfully reassured her that she was doing fine thanks. Her boss said to take as much time off as she needed but to just let her know when she had decided to come back to work. In the meantime they would get a temp in.

Over the following week, Caroline dealt with the multitude of decisions involved in arranging her parents' funeral. The company sent the obligatory wreath of flowers to her home, although nobody went to the funeral to represent her work colleagues. Even if they had, she would not have known they were there she was so deeply sad. She had never thought what her life would be like without her parents as they were both in good health and quite active in the community.

Not surprisingly, Owen didn't come to the funeral as he thought he might have to send flowers. To his way of thinking it was ridiculous to pay out all that good money for something that was going to be left on the ground on top of a pile of dirt. He did however phone her from work, once, of course at the company's expense, to enquire if she was okay. During this call he surprised Caroline by saying, "Oh well, at least you will have a fully paid house to live in." She thought this was rather heartless as her parents had only been gone such a short time and, to her way of thinking, having no mortgage was right at the bottom of her wish list.

Caroline eventually went to the solicitors to see what was in her parents' wills. Not surprisingly everything was left to her, but there was still a considerable amount to pay on the mortgage, as her father had only been able to make the minimum payments over the years. He had not been a big money earner, and her mother only worked part-time, so they had never managed to get ahead with the mortgage and certainly didn't think they would die before it was paid off. It was one of her father's dearest wishes to be mortgage free, but sadly he had not lived long enough to achieve this.

Caroline didn't earn enough to get a loan to pay out the balance of the mortgage and so with the solicitor's help she reluctantly decided to put the house up for sale. It had been a lovely family home, with her father always doing little odd jobs to keep it in tiptop condition. The furniture was a little old fashioned but it suited the house and gave it a cosy feel. Caroline hoped that whoever bought this home would look after it as lovingly as her parents had, but she knew she couldn't write that into the contract.

The house was emptied of their personal belongings and it was heart wrenching for her to open box after box of carefully preserved school reports with average grades, class photos, a misshapen piece of clay with MUM stamped into it, and so much more that was a capsule of her childhood. She put these minutiae of her life aside for the storage unit she had hired until she sorted out the rest of her life.

Hurry just lay on the lounge while Caroline dealt with getting the house ready for sale. He was grieving in his doggy way, because Stan and Sue had loved him too and Sue was always buying him a little treat with the weekly shopping. He could often be found at the front door as though he was listening for their car to come home, with perhaps the arrival of a juicy bone.

The first real estate agent who came to give an opinion on price, etc., was far too hearty for Caroline's liking. He didn't seem to be aware of the tragedy and remarked, "Well, it will be nice to get rid of this and move on with your life, won't it love?" He then went around the house making comments such as "old kitchen, that will get ripped out" and "original bathroom, that won't be a plus." After ten minutes Caroline asked him, in a very terse voice, to just leave, please. Even when angry, Caroline was always polite, as she had been taught.

She was aware that the house had not been modernised, but to her that was part of its charm. The second real estate agent was much more sympathetic to her plight and suggested a few little touches that wouldn't cost much and could add some dollars to the sale. He must have watched lots of TV programmes about how to market a property and even suggested hiring someone to come in and "dress" the home in a more modern way, preferably with rented furniture. All of this window dressing was going to cost Caroline money she didn't have, but if it got her a few more dollars then that would be worth the investment. She decided that she would seriously consider this strategy but would see what agent No. 3 had to say before making a final decision.

She was third time lucky. This agent was aware of Caroline's circumstances, both emotional and financial, and said that she would get the best price possible for her so that she could start a new life. They worked together on a marketing strategy that would cause her the least inconvenience but hopefully allow the maximum number of people to see the property. The only problem was that she had to keep Hurry out of the way when potential purchasers were viewing, as not everybody was a pet person. Caroline went in to see her kindly neighbours Wendy and Jim, and they agreed to let Hurry stay with them during viewings. They were retired so were on hand for daytime viewings when Caroline was at work. After a little more tweaking of the contract she signed the necessary papers and within days there was a big sign out the front advertising the property for sale and a forthcoming auction date.

Caroline felt very sad seeing it there and felt she had let her parents down by selling off the home they had lived in all their married life, but when it came down to finances, she just couldn't do it on her own. She just hoped her parents, wherever they were, would understand. She had done the best she could with presenting the house as had been advised and had decided to spend a little more money to bring it up to the standard that most buyers would expect. Emotionally it made a difference to her that with the rented furniture, rugs, lamps, and cushions it didn't really feel like her home anymore. It was now just somewhere she lived until it was sold and she could move on with her life.

There was quite a bit of interest in the property as it had "development potential," which is real estate speak for knock it down and build something else. However, most of the people who attended the viewings were older couples who had decided to downsize to a more modest home or young couples just starting out, who wanted a comfortable and affordable family home.

The day of the auction was fine and sunny, but Caroline and Hurry went next door to stay with Wendy and Jim. She knew the house had to be sold, but it felt like she had slammed a door shut on her childhood and all the fun and love she had shared with her parents. The auction proceeded without a hitch and the reserve price was reached quite quickly, coming down to a bidding war between an older couple and a young couple, but the young couple put in the last offer and the house was theirs.

Caroline came out of Wendy's place and met the new owners. They were a delightful couple and were looking forward to just doing up the place a bit but were certainly not going to knock down a property that had been so faithfully maintained. They just wanted to add their own touches with a new kitchen and bathroom, but they were delighted with their purchase and told Caroline how sorry they were for the reason the property was on the market.

When all the papers had been signed, Caroline went back into Wendy's to collect Hurry and dinner was waiting on the table for them all (except Hurry, who had a nice bone to chew). The auction was discussed, and the higher than expected price meant that Caroline would be able to rent a comfortable house in the neighbourhood so Hurry could be with her. There was no way she was going into a pet-free apartment and leaving her beloved dog behind. It crossed Caroline's mind that even though she had lived next door to Wendy and Jim all her life, she had never been as close to them as she was now and was very grateful for their help.

Chapter 5

Caroline had not returned to work while the house was on the market, and during that time she had not bothered to contact Owen. She was still quite hurt that he hadn't been any support to her through the dreadful time of her parents' deaths and funeral. His remark about her being lucky to be living in a fully paid house still rankled, mainly because she didn't think it was any of his business anyway. And she certainly didn't feel lucky.

Once the house was sold, Caroline used a small amount she had saved to pay the bond on leasing a very modest house on a bus route not far from the office. The hired furniture had been sent back so there was no point in staying in the house. Wendy and Jim helped her pack her modest belongings to wait for the removal van. She hadn't called on Owen when she was going through the trauma involved in putting away her old life and starting a new one because he always came up with excuses anyway.

When the house sale was finalised, her solicitor handed her a very nice cheque that he suggested she invest for a rainy day. It crossed Caroline's mind that no day could get any rainier than the day her parents died, but she kept her thoughts to herself as she knew the solicitor was kindly and meant well with his advice. She put the money away in a fixed deposit account so that it could grow with the annual interest, as she had no immediate plans for it.

Nobody from work had contacted her to see how she was managing and it was not as if the world would stop turning because Caroline Jensen was taking time off for a family tragedy. Caroline had never felt more alone in her whole life.

She hired a truck, driver, and helper to move her into her new home. She hadn't replaced her father's car so was without transport until the insurance money came through. Fortunately, the driver and his helper were very sympathetic to her plight and let Hurry sit up front with them. It was the highest he had ever been off the ground and wasn't too happy about the view, but he eventually settled down with some soft head patting and reassuring murmurs from Caroline.

She had kept some of her parents' furniture, as it was still in good condition except for Hurry's lounge, and she couldn't traumatise him by replacing this with a piece of cold leather at this stage of his life. She knew he wouldn't be with her for many more years, and it would be a sad day for here when Hurry went wherever good dogs go.

When Caroline returned to work, people were kind and enquired about how she was doing and when she answered, "I'm okay thanks" they would reply, "That's good" and go on their way. It was really just lip service, and she accepted it as such. Owen made his way past her office during the morning and asked, "So, how is it going?"

"I am coping" she replied quietly. "I just have to get on with it " She was disappointed that he didn't seem to be any more interested in her sore heart than anyone else.

"Yes, that's probably for the best. You will get over it in time." That was easy for him to say, as it wasn't his parents who had been so supportive and loving.

On her first Friday back it was pub night, but that was the last thing Caroline felt like doing. Owen quietly suggested they give it a miss "Let's go somewhere quiet for a coffee or a meal, if you feel like it "

During the meal he asked her how she liked living in her own house? Her reply rather caught him by surprise when she told him the house had been auctioned because she couldn't afford to pay the mortgage. Only the rapid raising of his eyebrows gave him away as he hardly missed a beat. "Well then, what are you going to do with the profits from your parents' estate?" She was rather annoyed with his blunt questioning, and when she told him it would only be a small amount he was obviously disappointed. The thought flashed through Caroline's mind *what has it got to do with you anyway*? She had never been in the habit of discussing her personal life with anyone, least of all a workmate, albeit one with whom she shared a meal now and then.

It was obvious from the look on Owen's face that he wasn't impressed when she also told him she had moved into a small rented house not far from work because she couldn't have Hurry in an apartment. He more or less told her she was wasting what money she had just because of the dog. Caroline's rather terse reply, "It's my money and my dog, so I will spend it how I want," caused Owen's lips to tighten as he wasn't used to being challenged.

He was somewhat shocked by Caroline's spunk, and he was far from impressed by her reaction. He thought Hurry was past his Use By date anyway. Owen thought other people's animals were a waste of time and money, and he would never consider organising his household around one.

Caroline was a bit surprised when at the end of the meal Owen said that her half of the bill was $15.35, but she handed over the money anyway. In her mind it wasn't a real date or anything like that, just work friends sharing a meal. In Owen's mind, he wasn't going to pay for someone else's meal, no matter who they were. Caroline didn't know yet just how mean with money Owen could be.

In the absence of any other invitations, Owen and Caroline continued to see each other over the next two years, usually for dinner once a week at a cheap restaurant of his choice where she paid half the bill. When the restaurant had a two-for-one deal, he was so happy you would think he had won the lottery. There was no halving the bill on that occasion. He had the voucher so he got the free meal, and Caroline paid for the full-price one. It worked for him. If he could get free tickets for something, no matter what it was, he would suggest they go. This often resulted in sitting through plays where at times there were only twenty people in the audience. The point was it was free; however, it was usually awful as well.

Over the two years chaste kisses on the cheek by Owen had progressed to a swift collision of the lips. There was no tonsil hockey in his handbook of lovemaking. An arm around Caroline's shoulders to guide her through a doorway or pulling her arm through his as they walked across the road was about as romantic as it got. Caroline would not have been averse to a little more intimacy and romance but thought that Owen would be horrified if she showed any initiative. She suspected that he would think she was much too forward, as he was the man and he would call the shots on how far things went and when.

Owen didn't drink very much, usually because it cost money, but one Friday pub night he got caught up in a round of drinks, and he and Caroline were quite inebriated by the time they went out into the cold air; neither of them had eaten much, except a few potato chips. Caroline talked Owen into taking a taxi to her place as it was the closest and therefore would cost less. The idea that it would be cheaper was the swinging vote and so they arrived at Caroline's front door, a little the worse for wear.

Caroline suggested he come in and have some black coffee to sober up a bit and he could sleep on the lounge. Even in his alcoholic state he checked that it wasn't Hurry's lounge he was going to sleep on and was reassured when Caroline explained she had two lounges, one of which was a sofa bed, and that he would be quite comfortable.

The sofa bed was pulled out and Caroline got a quilt, sheets and pillows from the drawer underneath it. While she was doing this, the coffee was perking, and by the time it was ready in the kitchen, Owen was asleep and snoring. She quietly let Hurry out for his nighttime toilet, and when he slowly made his way back inside on his poor sore legs, she settled him on his lounge and went off to her room. It made her sad to see Hurry becoming feebler, and she suspected his days were numbered, but she loved that dog more than any human on earth.

Before her eyes were open in the morning there was a rattling of cups in the kitchen, and for just a moment she forgot that Owen had spent the night in the lounge room. She chastely pulled on her rather old and unattractive woolly dressing gown that was decorated with unidentifiable food stains, probably from supper snacks when she curled up on the lounge, and made her way into the kitchen. Owen had found the instant coffee, a cheap brand he was happy to note, and had tipped a spoonful in each china mug. He added water and then enquired if Caroline wanted milk added.

She was a bit embarrassed about her dressing gown, and Owen was crumpled from sleeping in his clothes. Yesterday's brown suit didn't look so good this morning. They sat sipping their coffee on either side of the old painted kitchen table that had done duty for years in her parents' house.

Owen looked awkward, and his unshaved face, combined with a hangover, didn't lend themselves to any romantic interlude. After he had drunk some coffee, he tipped the rest down the sink and made a hasty exit. As he was leaving to head for the bus stop, he instructed Caroline not to let anyone at work know he had stayed at her house because he had his reputation to protect. *"And what about my reputation?*

The next time they saw each other was at work on Monday. They were quite shy with each other, and Owen sent Caroline a message through their in-house email to see if she would like to go out to dinner on Wednesday night as there was a special price on at the local pub. She accepted, and they agreed to meet at the pub so no one would know they were going out together. It escaped both of them that no one would be the least bit interested and would more than likely be amazed that either of them had a date, even if it was with each other. The two most socially inept people in the office were just made for each other.

Chapter 6

Caroline was now twenty-seven years old and felt that life was passing her by. She had been asked at work to donate to Tanya's engagement gift, Amelia's baby shower, and so on and she never refused. However, it did not escape her that even though she was contributing to gifts for occasions, she was never asked to the event itself.

Owen was very canny when it came to putting in for gifts. He just said that he didn't have any cash on him and wouldn't be going to the bank until … and stated a date that was past the occasion being collected for. His hard-earned money wasn't leaving his hands for some event that he would never get to be a part of.

Caroline wasn't sure how she felt about Owen. She didn't really have much experience with what made the opposite sex tick. She didn't know if they were actually in a "relationship" or if they were just two people who went out together in the absence of any other offers.

On analysing her feelings, she decided that there were certain qualities about Owen that she liked. He was good-living (or was that, not really living). He was always neat and tidy (even if he wore the same colours all the time, but that wasn't a crime). He was careful with money (or did that come down to the fact that he was actually mean?).

He liked animals (or at least he asked her if Hurry was still alive). Was this enough to base a whole life upon?

She had nobody to ask, and in the absence of siblings, she just had to work it out for herself. She didn't want to spend the rest of her life alone and she would like at least one child, so where to now? Should she stop going out with Owen and try to find someone else? She reasoned that up to age twenty-five she hadn't had much success, so why would that change now that she was older? Travelling didn't interest her; mainly because she had no one to travel with and baulked at using her savings to pay for a single supplement. What was she to do with the rest of her life?

The day arrived when Hurry didn't wake in the morning and Caroline was devastated. He had reached the grand old age of sixteen and her last link with her previous life had gone in the night. Caroline rang the vet who had looked after Hurry all his life and he came as soon as he could. She had left the front door unlocked and sat on the floor in her daggy dressing gown with her beloved dog's head in her lap, saying her goodbyes, and dripping her tears down onto his face. She had previously made arrangements with the vet for how she wanted Hurry cremated and some ashes returned to her, so there was no need for her to go over that now. The vet lightly knocked on the front door before letting himself into her home, gently lifting Hurry from her lap into a blanket and taking him out to the van.

Caroline was inconsolable. She had never really had time to grieve for her parents because there was so much to do in such a short time by herself, but now the tears flowed like a river. She eventually got up from the floor, made herself a cup of tea, and rang work to call in sick. There was no point in telling them the reason. They would just think she was nuttier than they already did, so she pleaded a cold and after an hour or so of crying she certainly sounded believable on that score.

Owen phoned from work during the day "How come you are not at work today? They said you had a cold but you were alright yesterday"

"Hurry passed away last night and I was too upset to come in today so I made the excuse that I was sick."

"Well he was old and probably lived longer than he should have" replied Owen in a matter of fact way. "You will be able to get on with your life now. Anyway, see you tomorrow".

I already had a life thanks Owen and I will miss Hurry for the rest of my days.

Caroline went back to work the next day with red-rimmed eyes, but those who cared to notice just assumed she still had her cold. Owen made the comment that she probably should have stayed home until she felt better, but from where Caroline was standing that could be years. You just didn't lose a pet you had had for almost half your life and then when it was gone just "feel better." Owen did however ask her if she would like to have lunch with him, and she was amazed when he paid the bill without tallying up her share. Caroline considered that maybe he wasn't without empathy after all but just had difficulty showing his feelings.

She hated going home to her empty quiet house and decided it was time to make another move. The money from her parents' house sale had been invested while she rented the cottage so she decided to set herself up in a unit complex where she would be amongst more people, maybe even some younger ones with whom she might make friends.

Caroline knew how much she could afford to rent a unit and found a small "one-bedroom studio apartment" (real estate speak for bedroom-like cupboard and lounge room nonexistent) not far from work. It was "a blank canvas," another real estate term for "bland and boring coloured walls, floors and fittings."

It was fun shopping for new furniture, but she was careful to only a few buy small pieces, as she had kept some from her parent's house.

Since Caroline had been living on her own, albeit for a relatively short time, she liked the idea of having colourful modern appliances and had even splurged on a bright red kettle and matching toaster to give her monochrome kitchen a spot of colour. It made her happy each morning when she blearily went for her first cup of tea or coffee and the toaster gently elevated the beautifully even brown squares of bread to just the right height for her fingers to grasp the top of them. It was such a small thing to not have the toaster make a loud crash just to get the toast high enough to burn one's fingers when trying to free it.

She had never felt so lonely in her entire life, but from somewhere deep within her soul, she managed to find the energy to go on and make a new world for herself. She missed Hurry enormously, but nothing could replace him, and she wouldn't even try. It was sad when she saw his lounge thrown into the back of a rubbish truck, and she couldn't help but shed a tear. It was cutting the last tie with her previous life, but Caroline decided to sell off what was left of her parents' furniture, as it just wouldn't fit in her new "compact" living quarters.

The next thing to do was get a car as the insurance money from her father's car had eventually been paid. Caroline started looking on the Internet, which wasn't really helpful because she didn't know what sort of car to look for or how much she should pay. There was no point consulting Owen because he thought cars were a waste of money.

After a few Saturdays catching buses to areas where car yards sat side by side, she decided to go for a small new one. She reasoned that she would get a warranty in case anything went wrong and she wouldn't be buying someone else's trouble. She knew her dollar limit and was quite firm, unusual for Caroline, when the salesman tried to option up her choice. The more he pushed the more she pushed and she finally found a small two-door car in electric blue with soft grey seats. She got it for the price she had stated at the outset and paid her deposit. She was to pick it up in three days.

Caroline was so pleased with herself. This was her first big purchase. She had done it! She could hardly wait to show it to Owen and hoped he would be as pleased with her purchase. He wasn't.

On Wednesday she asked Owen if he would come with her to collect her car. "Collect your what?" he exploded. She reeled back a bit but explained that she had always planned to replace her father's car and had now done so. When Owen found out that the car was brand new, Caroline thought he was going to have a heart attack. His face went red and the veins in his neck popped out to an alarming extent and she thought his eyebrows would disappear up into his already-receding hairline. "We will have a look at it," he stated, "but if I think it is a waste of money you will have to cancel the sale. I can't have my future wife wasting our money."

"Future wife? Where did that come from? Was that a proposal or just a way to get me to cancel the sale and put the money back in my bank account? Our money? Since when?"

All these thoughts whirled around in Caroline's head as she waited for the colour in Owen's face to subside, which it did after a few minutes. Caroline thought it was going to be an interesting trip to the car yard and whatever events followed the viewing of her new car that she had secretly christened Betty.

Thirty minutes later Caroline was signing her name on the dotted line while Owen was off kicking tyres and peering in windows. She had told him she was going to the ladies and to wait for her in the car yard. She reasoned that if he got to the papers before she did he would make such a fuss that it would be embarrassing. She was handed the keys to Betty, which was parked just outside the showroom doors in sparkling splendour, and called to Owen, "I am ready to go now."

He turned around and looked furious. He strode across the car park and with his face about thirty centimetres away from hers he exploded, "You tricked me and signed the papers!" Caroline was on a bit of a high so didn't take too much notice of his anger. If she had, it would have given her an insight into what was ahead.

Caroline and Owen left with Caroline at the wheel and Owen sulking in the passenger seat. "Isn't this wonderful?" she enthused into the palpable silence.

"What?" snarled Owen.

"Being able to drive places without having to catch buses and trains, especially when it is wet and cold. It is only a small engine so it won't cost much to run."

There was no conversation forthcoming from the passenger's side, so the next time she stopped at a red light, Caroline reached forward and turned the radio up just a little so there was at least some sound in the car.

When she pulled up outside Owen's front door, she felt as though she had had a punch to the solar plexus when she realised the previous time she had done this was the day she drove him home from hospital, and that it was the last day of her parents' life. It diminished the joy she felt in owning Betty but didn't completely eliminate it. She was hurt that he hadn't been generous enough to share in her joy, but one of her father's favourite sayings had been "Expect nothing and you won't be disappointed."

On the way to her newly furnished apartment, she mulled over the comments Owen had made about "his future wife spending money." Was he thinking of asking her to marry him? Owen was not one to be rushed in important decisions.

She caught the bus to work as usual the next day, and when she saw Owen in the office, he seemed to be in a better mood, which was a relief to her. He sent her an email message asking if she would like to go out Saturday night to dinner and/or a movie. She was still a little hurt at how he had exploded about the car, and after all it was her money not his, so she left it for a few hours before she responded, "Yes."

Between Thursday and Saturday, Owen and Caroline made arrangements that she would pick him up at his home about five and they would go to a local pizza place where they had a special "dine by 5.30 and out by 7 for half price." Even though Owen disapproved of Caroline buying Betty, he wasn't too proud to ride in the passenger seat and be driven to their destination. Best of all, it wasn't costing him any bus or taxi fares. There was no way he was putting in for the petrol, because after all, it wasn't his car.

For quite a few weeks, even including the surprise and unwelcome purchase of Betty, Owen had been weighing up his options. Here was a girl who was ready for marriage and family, and so was he. She had some money in the bank and now "they" had a car between them. He had his mother's mortgage-free house and they both had jobs, not a huge combined income but enough to get by. He thought it was probably time he popped the question. He was fairly sure the answer would be "Yes."

After they left the pizza place before seven, he suggested they go for a drive down to the beach as he had something he wanted to talk to her about. She was a little nervous as she thought he was going to go on about the money she'd wasted on Betty. She was enjoying her newfound freedom and so loved her little blue car. It was fondly garaged each evening and she washed it every weekend in the community car-washing area at the units. She even got to see some of the spunky topless young men who also washed their cars, but none of them had a car as small as Betty. She had mentioned to Owen the guys and their black, silver or red cars that thundered out of the underground garages and roared up the street as though they were heading for the Indianapolis 500 starting line.

Owen hadn't liked the "tone" of what she was telling him about the other inhabitants of the unit block, and mentioned that he hoped they weren't half naked when they were car washing. They were, but

Caroline wasn't going to confirm this part of the conversation and have Owen go off on another of his moral campaigns. She could look, even if she couldn't touch.

After about thirty minutes Caroline pulled into the deserted parking area at the local beach. It was the first time they had been alone in a car in such a desolate spot. It wasn't long before Owen launched into his pitch.

"Now Caroline," he started off in a nervous voice "we have been seeing each other for about three years now, and I think it is time we got married." Caroline was a little taken aback, but given the barren future she envisaged for herself she replied, "I think that would be lovely, Owen." And so the "deal" was sealed, or should that be "fate"?

There didn't seem to be anything else forthcoming from Owen, so Caroline started the car and headed back in the direction of his home. No more was said on the way home about an engagement or marriage plans so she once again pulled up outside his door. He got out and said, "We will talk about this later and make plans." Caroline just nodded; he shut the door and was gone into the night.

When she got home she opened a bottle of wine, not so much to celebrate her apparent engagement but to go back over the night and examine her feelings about this person with whom she was going to share the rest of her life. She wasn't bubbling over with joy, but she wasn't unhappy either. Perhaps the word *perplexed* would cover how she felt. The sadness crept in when she realised that there would be no parents at their wedding and wondered whom they would invite to the church and reception. It would probably be a small wedding, she mused, as Owen wasn't one to make a fuss, except when he'd found out about Betty.

She was surprised when the bottle of wine was empty, as she hadn't been aware of the constant sipping. She felt a bit light-headed but wasn't sure if that was the wine, the excitement (maybe not), or the anticipation of the honeymoon and its natural progression into sexual delights—or so she had overheard the latest bride relaying to those gathered around the water cooler. Caroline couldn't quite imagine some of the positions that were being discussed, but she supposed they must be possible. There was no way she was going to ask and then be laughed at for her inexperience. She was probably the first twenty-eight-year-old virgin to ever work in the company, judging by the age and experiences of her female colleagues.

She felt a bit hung over the next morning, but she wasn't going to impart that bit of information to Owen when he phoned her on his mobile, which really surprised her. It was the first time he had ever done that, but as it was Sunday he wasn't at work so that was his only choice. Not being one to use up his credit he briefly asked Caroline what time she could come over to his place to discuss their wedding and would she bring something for lunch? She agreed to twelve-thirty and confirmed that she would stop for some food on the way.

Just before twelve-thirty, Caroline pulled up in Owen's driveway and unloaded her purchases. He came halfway down the path to meet her and helped carry the groceries into the kitchen. She was surprised to see a bottle of inexpensive bubbly, definitely not French champagne, in the sink with ice cubes halfway up the sides of the bottle. Owen's mother had apparently not had an ice bucket stashed amongst the Royal Albert china.

He motioned for her to sit down as he unpacked the deli items she had brought with her. "Thanks for picking up the things for lunch. I am glad you didn't buy expensive meat like ham" he commented. Caroline didn't bother to enlighten him that she had bought what she liked to eat and ham wasn't one of those things. He got the lunch organised and went in search of a wine glass, but could only find two thick glass tumblers. Given the quality of the wine, the tumblers were probably appropriate. Waterford crystal would have been wasted.

Caroline was gazing around the room and realised that the kitchen was probably the original, and the house was built in the 1930s. It was badly in need of refurbishment, but she doubted that Owen would spend money on it before he put it on the market and they moved into a place of their mutual choosing. She was daydreaming about what sort of place they could share when Owen interrupted with "Lunch is ready" and they proceeded to eat. He poured her a tumbler of wine and she almost choked on the first mouthful. It tasted like vinegar and very poor quality vinegar at that! This was not going well.

Owen hadn't taken a mouthful yet, but was somewhat surprised at the look on Caroline's face. He was definitely not a wine connoisseur, but he had read somewhere that wine got better as it got older; therefore, he reasoned that as this bottle was left over from his mother's funeral it should be tip top by now. But not if it only cost $2.99 in the first place! They mutually decided that there must have been something wrong with the wine when it was bottled a decade ago and water would have to do instead.

As Caroline was halfway through her lunch Owen started outlining the plans for their wedding, but it was a different plan to the one that Caroline had in mind.

"Now Caroline" he started off "Probably the first thing to do is organise an engagement ring."

"That would be nice" replied Caroline but was dumfounded when Owen began again about his idea.

"We can either use my mother's engagement ring, or your mother's one, if she left it behind. It is pointless wasting money when we already have rings that can be utilised, don't you think?" Caroline was only partly listening to Owen's ideas. Her idea of going hand in hand to a jeweller's and having the assistant take tray after tray of sparkling gems from the display case, Owen gently placing her choice on her finger, while he gazed at her adoringly and reached into his wallet to bring out his platinum credit card … Oh yes, that idea just evaporated like the morning mist when she realised he was talking about second-hand.

Owen felt rather pleased with himself. In his mind Caroline could choose her engagement ring, as every woman should be able to do. She would have the choice between her mother's ring or his mother's ring. However, he totally missed the point that either way she was going to get a second-hand, old-style ring because there had been no intention on Owen's part of having it remade. Caroline just hoped that one of the rings would fit or she would be forever relegated to having one of those little metal clips pinching the back of her finger to reduce the size of the circle.

Oh yes, he was moving onto the wedding. Caroline envisaged floating down the aisle towards her love (or Owen in this case) in a dress that she had chosen from an amazing display at a city shop well known for its splendid and rather expensive dresses, her headpiece a tiara and her veil floating out three metres behind her …

"Sorry, what were you saying?" answered Caroline.

"I said, do you want to be married in the morning or the afternoon because we will have to try and choose a time at the Registry Office."

The church wedding had just gone the way of the store bought engagement ring.

"Oh, morning will do," answered Caroline. It would give more time for the reception and make it take longer to get to the honeymoon bit, which was the part of the day she was very anxious about.

"We won't invite guests because there really isn't anyone that we would want there. We can just use the staff at the Registry Office as our witnesses." Not a question, just a statement. "And there is no reason to have a reception because it is just a waste of money."

Caroline was beginning to think that there was hardly much point to her being there either. Maybe she would get to choose the honeymoon as she had so far struck out on the sparkling new engagement ring, the floating white dress, and the reception where she would be the centre of attention. Perhaps she and Owen needed to talk about this in a bit more detail, but then she realised he was speaking again.

"Pardon?" Owen was getting a little tetchy by now as he had realised that his captive audience wasn't as captive as he'd thought, and she was off on some mental journey of her own. Most inconsiderate as he was trying to give her a day she would remember.

"Honeymoon?" Caroline enquired.

"Yes, honeymoon was what I was talking about," replied Owen in a terse voice, "while you were off with the pixies." I wouldn't mind going to a nice island resort somewhere off Queensland, or Fiji would be nice." She thought Owen had a chicken bone stuck in his neck as he started to splutter and almost lost his breath. "An island resort or Fiji. Are you mad, woman? Do you know how much those places charge?" Well, Caroline had never really thought about the cost because she naively figured that Owen would be paying for it and after all she had lost three out of four rounds in this discussion.

After he calmed down and got his breath back he said, "I thought we might just spend the one night at a place in town. They are three-star but close to transport, and we can get Sunday night for half price with a basket breakfast included."

"But we are getting married on a Saturday, aren't we?" she questioned.

"Yes, but we can spend Saturday night at my place and then get the bus into the city after lunch on Sunday because we can't check in until two unless we pay extra."

Caroline saw her dreams of an island honeymoon travelling along the same mist-shrouded pathway as the sparkling new engagement ring, white bridal gown, church wedding, and reception. It was Owen 4 and Caroline 0.

Chapter 7

Since "they" had decided to marry, Owen had pulled out all stops to get Caroline to move into "his" place but she'd resisted with all her might. She didn't want to use the dishes and rose-patterned china that her fiancé's mother had stored in the cupboards for special occasions. The stove was positively ancient, and she was scared of gas jets. She liked the nice flat black glass electric type that were so easy to clean and didn't have little blue and pink flames licking at your saucepan. She very much doubted that her visually appealing shiny red appliances would fit into the décor of Owen's kitchen.

She was having second thoughts about this wedding. She felt short changed about the whole process, but had no previous experiences to compare it with. She tried to reassure herself that no matter what or where the ceremony was held, at the end of the day she would be Mrs Owen Brewster.

Is that what I really want, or, am I just scared that I won't get another offer?

She was also aware that she would have to live in a house she passionately disliked. It was so old and tired, but it was unlikely that

Owen was going to do anything to freshen it up either. Paying for paint was not something he had done as yet and probably never would.

She could stand her ground and try to negotiate that they live in her apartment, but to Owen that would be financial suicide because they would be paying rent when they had a "perfectly good house" to live in. His mother's old apron was still hanging behind the kitchen door and had faded where the high folds of the creases were in the weak sunlight each day. It was, on the whole, depressing to even think about it—so she didn't. Or, at least, she tried not to think about it.

They had decided to get married two months from his "proposal" and time was getting away. She needed to buy a new dress, nothing too outlandish as Owen thought something she could also wear to work would fit the bill.

What bride wears her wedding dress to work?

Nonetheless, she went shopping and bought a fairly plain suit in a turquoise colour that she thought would look nice with her dark hair and blue eyes. Hats were old fashioned, and she wasn't one for wearing those silly bits of feathers and net that seemed to be the look of the moment. A nice clutch bag and high heels completed her conservative outfit. When she looked in the mirror she was disappointed, as she did indeed look like she was going to work—and about as happy.

Owen was wearing one of his brown suits—no surprise there. He decided to wear his newest one, not that anyone would know which one that was, as they all looked the same to Caroline. He did, however, allow her to buy him a new tie and was a bit dubious when he saw that it had a very narrow stripe of turquoise to match her suit. He rejected, out of hand, the socks that matched the tie. He told Caroline, in no uncertain terms, that his ankles were not going to be clad in socks with a splash of blue like a downed peacock. Caroline thought that description was a bit over the top but went along with his choice anyway. It was more important that they were both happy on the Big Day. She didn't realise it then but she was setting up a pattern of subservience that would permeate their marriage and cause her so much unhappiness.

She had chosen to wear her mother's diamond engagement ring for sentimental reasons. She was a bit flabbergasted that she not only had to supply her own engagement ring but pay for the resizing and cleaning as well. One night, about two weeks before they were married, he presented her with her revamped engagement ring. Owen had taken it for resizing and cleaning so it only cost HER $25.00.

He looked so proud that he had managed to produce a ring that had been brought back to its original glory, even if it was a few decades old. As he knew her finger size, he had taken it upon himself to go to Cash Converters and get a 9ct gold plain wedding ring—18ct was twice the price—and get it polished at the same time as the engagement ring. He wasn't planning on wearing a wedding ring. Real men didn't do that.

She hadn't told anyone at work that she was engaged and even though it was old fashioned, she was proud to wear her mother's ring and hoped she would be as happy as her parents had been. She wasn't friendly enough with any of the girls to have a giggle session about the upcoming nuptials, but her female boss noticed the ring on her finger and enquired who was the lucky man? When Caroline identified Owen, she said "Really?" and then followed with "What on Earth made you choose him?"

Caroline didn't really have any reply so she just put her eyes down and replied, "We get along okay. He's really quite nice once you get to know him" She didn't see her boss's eyebrows go up and her eyes roll.

During the fortnight before the wedding, Caroline had reluctantly given in and was moving to Owen's house. He had assured her it would be "their" house but she had serious doubts. She had been backed into a corner because Owen refused to rent anywhere. He could not, or would not, understand her trepidation. The first thing she was going to do was get rid of that damned apron behind the kitchen door. She felt as though it haunted the kitchen. She had never met Owen's mother, and she was probably a very nice lady, but it was a reminder that a woman had been the custodian of this house before her. Perhaps his mother had had more say than she suspected she would be having.

Owen helped her pack her belongings and transport them in Betty to her new "home." They were to share the bedroom that Owen's parents had occupied for all those decades and she was horrified when she realised he hadn't even bought a new bed and mattress for the start of their married life. When she mentioned that it would be nice to start afresh, his reply was typical. "Do you know how much they cost?" She then suggested that as she had a new mattress in her rented abode, they might get rid of his parents' one and transfer hers across to their new bedroom. It was then she discovered that the old double bed his parents had installed had very different measurements to the queen-size mattress that Caroline owned.

Owen suggested that they sell Caroline's mattress on eBay, using the computer at work of course, and put the money towards new sheets and quilt, which would freshen the whole bedroom. Caroline really didn't want to sleep on some old mattress that was probably close on half a century old, no matter how it was covered up with new sheets and quilts. It was a dilemma for her. She felt as though she was constantly negotiating to have some of her own possessions in this house she was going to share with her fiancé in less than two weeks.

She was committed to this relationship and would make the best of it. She had to decide what was more important to her, having her possessions around her or starting a new life with Owen. She really had difficulty making up her mind and there was no one else she could ask.

Her wedding suit hung in its pristine plastic bag over her bedroom door; she had bought some new makeup and underwear, sensible of course as she didn't want Owen commenting on wasting money on lacy bits and pieces, shoes, and a bag. A wedding gift collection was taken up at work, but since Owen had never put in for anything it was a very small yield, although sufficient to buy a K-mart dinner set with large blue flowers in the centre of each piece. It was unattractive to say the least, but Caroline tried to make the best of it. She was gracious when it was presented to them both on the Friday afternoon, the day before their wedding, but they weren't asked on that occasion to go to the pub so they took their gift to Owen's place.

It was supposed to be unlucky for the bride to see her groom on their wedding day, but Caroline really didn't have any choice. She had moved out of her rented unit, which had been relet, and most of her possessions had been relegated to the storage unit she had on a short lease, including Hurry's ashes. Owen said it was creepy for them to be on the mantelpiece. The only things of hers that had been moved into "their" house were her clothes and personal belongings.

She was rather surprised when, on the eve of their wedding, Owen made up a bed for her on the lounge. She was still a virgin and wondered if he was too. They had never really discussed any previous relationships, which on Caroline's part would not have taken long, but Owen had not mentioned anyone he had taken out. This could just be a gentleman not besmirching a lady's reputation, but it was a bit weird to Caroline's way of thinking.

Within the next twenty-four hours she would be Owen's wife so whatever had or had not happened was in the past and she was looking forward to their future—or should have been.

Is it wrong to get married just because I am lonely?

Her lack of siblings, cousins or girlfriends to talk to about her fears of an intimate relationship made her nervous about the wedding night as she didn't know what to really expect. She would just have to go along with whatever Owen wanted to do.

Her mother had never been very forthcoming about sex, but Caroline had absorbed her attitude that it was part of a loving marriage. She understood the basics of the male and female anatomy, thanks to the rather lurid descriptions around the water cooler, and she had researched the subject on the Internet ... but was left with the impression that there should be some feelings in there somewhere. She liked Owen and thought he would look after her, but apart from that she was in the dark.

She approached the morning of her wedding day with great trepidation. Owen woke her with a cup of tea brought from the kitchen to her bed on the lounge and he was modestly clothed in an almost floor-length dressing gown with a silk-thread quilted waist tie. He looked like an old grandfather with his twenty-four-hour beard that was not nearly as dark as his thinning hair and he was only just over thirty years old!

Caroline checked that she could have first shower, as she didn't want to disrupt his morning routine, even if it was Saturday and his wedding day. She correctly suspected that Owen had his routine and preferred to stick to it. Another negotiation took place, and she got to have her shower after Owen. She wanted to wash her hair so that she looked as good as she could even if no photographer was hired. They were just going to use her small camera and ask the staff at the Registry Office to take a few pictures.

The hot water tank was so small that the water went cool only a few minutes after Caroline had soaped up her hair with shampoo. By the time she got to the conditioning of her hair the water was less than room temperature, and she was shivering as she wrapped the single thin towel around her. She then noticed that the towel had "MUM" embroidered on it and in that moment she knew she would have to go to the storage shed and release her towel with *Caroline* written in script. It was her small way of stamping her presence on the household.

She wasn't sure where to get dressed because her clothes were hanging over the door of "Owen's" bedroom and she had forgotten to bring her underwear into the bathroom. She pulled the towel around her and covered as much as she could. It was then a dash down the hall to collect her clothes and another dash back to the bathroom from where she emerged completely dressed. Her hair was still wet because she had forgotten to bring her dryer and this necessitated a quick towel dry of her shoulder-length hair. Fortunately she had been given beautiful hair that responded well to not much fussing. Dried off, brushed into place, and pulled up on top of her head, it gave her a somewhat bridal look.

Owen had decided that she didn't need a bouquet because they were only getting married in a Registry Office, which took a maximum of twenty minutes. Her last act of defiance as a single woman was to go out to the garden, find a small pink flower, and pin it to her clutch purse. She was not getting married without flowers. One flower was a pathetic excuse for a bouquet, but it was the best she could do on short notice. Owen took one look at her bag, recognised that he had been defied, and turned abruptly on his heel, heading for the door.

"Are you ready to leave?" he enquired in a frosty tone of voice. Owen did not like to have his wishes thwarted.

Great start to a wedding day.

Caroline smiled briefly at Owen as she passed him in the doorway and walked slowly towards Betty, parked at the kerb; ready to transport the bride and groom to their wedding. On this occasion Owen chose to drive and Caroline was relegated to the passenger seat.

A parking space was found close to the Registry Office and they proceeded to join their lives in holy matrimony, whatever that meant. It was a lovely sunny morning, but for Caroline there were no girlfriends gathered around giggling and laughing as their hair was done and makeup applied. No dresses were hanging on doors with shoes below waiting for the bridesmaid to put them on. No photographer was knocking on the door asking, "Are you girls ready yet?" No anxious mother was in the kitchen trying to get the girls to eat something before the champagne was handed around to celebrate this day in her daughter's life. There was no nervous father waiting in the wings, dressed in a new suit with a scratchy collar on his starched shirt and a tie that threatened to cut off his air supply. No bouquets had been stored in a neighbour's refrigerator to keep them fresh until required. No highly polished limousines were pulling up out front with the chauffeur laying out a red carpet for the bride to walk safely to her transport, with her father on her arm. There were no neighbours lining the footpath to see this girl they had known since a small child go to her wedding.

I really miss you today Mum and Dad and I hope you are together, wherever you are. Please wish me well in my new life.

Owen parked the car and told Caroline that they had arrived at their destination. With consternation she looked out the window to see a dreary brick and stone building with a black marble block over the entrance engraved with Registry of Births, Deaths and Marriages. They had it all covered. From arrival in the world to despatch from it could be recorded in this building. That did nothing to elevate Caroline's mood from nervous to ecstatic, the level where she thought she should be on this important day in her life. *Am I really doing the right thing?* But by the time this thought had passed through her brain, Owen was taking her arm and guiding her through the doorway with the black marble plaque above it.

She repeated the words required of her, signed where she was directed, thanked the strangers who had witnessed this occasion and taken some photos, and walked behind Owen back out into the sunlight. She was not really in the moment, but there was no turning back now. Her life before Owen was gone and she was stuck in a limbo between what was and what was going to be. She was now Owen's wife, for better or worse, and she hoped it was going to be the former.

Owen and Caroline left the Registry Office and walked back to Betty, who would transfer them back to "their" home. Again, Owen decided to drive and Caroline took the passenger seat. They pulled up in the driveway and he suggested she open the front door.

"Aren't you going to carry me over the threshold?" she joked.

"Certainly not. I would look ridiculous." And that was the end of that. Married life had apparently started but not with any great expectations on Caroline's part.

The front door was closed, and the newly married couple headed for the kitchen. This was the only place in the house where they had both been without any embarrassment. Owen asked, "Would you like a cup of tea?"

"A glass of wine would be nice, just to celebrate."

"I think three pm is a little early for a drink, don't you?" Owen admonished Caroline. She was a little taken aback. It was their wedding day after all and surely a celebration was in order? Wasn't it? He apparently didn't think so and went to the cupboard to get the dreaded rose-patterned china down, which meant a cup of tea.

Oh, for goodness sake, live on the edge occasionally.

They watched television for a few hours, took a frozen pizza out and heated it in the oven and at nine Owen suggested that they finish their tea and go to bed. Caroline wasn't at all sure what was expected of her, but when she went down the hall to "their" bedroom she found Owen was in the bathroom changing into his pyjamas. What was she supposed to do? Should she do the same, after he came out of course?

After a lot of "excuse me" and "no, after you" they were both in their nightwear, teeth cleaned and flossed, and in the double bed that had belonged to Owen's parents, Caroline's bed having been sold to a couple on eBay.

Owen had plunged the room into darkness by turning off his bedside lamp as soon as Caroline's back hit the mattress. What followed was a lot of fumbling, and "oh sorry, did that hurt?" and "no, that's fine" until the final culmination—Caroline wide-awake.

She asked herself, "Was that it?" *Suppose so.* "Well, that was a bit of a disappointment. I am sure what they talk about around the water cooler at work is not as lukewarm as that was." She was now Mrs Owen Brewster and had better get used to her new life.

Chapter 8

The wedding night was over, and at eight the next morning Caroline awoke to the sound of cups and saucers rattling in the kitchen. Owen appeared in the doorway, clad in his usual floor-length dressing gown, with a cup and saucer in each hand. He sat on the edge of the bed and Caroline had to move over to accommodate him. He handed her the pink rose-patterned cup of tea and kept the blue one for himself.

"Did you enjoy last night?" he enquired with a barely concealed smirk.

"It was alright," Caroline answered quietly, not looking at him.

Owen appeared shocked. "What do you mean, alright?" he asked with an edge to his voice. In his mind he had been quite a stud and performed as any grateful wife would expect. The fact that he had never actually had sex before, and therefore had nothing to base his judgement of success or otherwise on, was irrelevant.

All that Caroline was aware of was that she had spent the night sleeping next to a male who snored with the volume of a thunderstorm and she had slept on the wet side of the bed. It would be her doing the washing later, she was sure of that. *Am I happy? What is happy?* She was married, and this was her life from now on, no matter what.

Owen took their empty cups from the bedroom and told her that she had better get up, shower, and get dressed as they were leaving for their honeymoon about one, but they would have lunch first. He expressed the opinion that Caroline should prepare a larger-than-usual midday meal so that they could just have a toasted sandwich for dinner, as it wouldn't cost as much.

Caroline's usual wardrobe was rather meagre as she only went to work and then home, with the occasional night at the pub—in her previous life. Owen suggested that she wear her wedding suit and when they got to the hotel to make sure she mentioned they were on their honeymoon and they might get an upgrade, or at least a bottle of champagne. She hoped that if they did score a bottle of bubbly it was better than the one left over from his mother's funeral!

Before getting ready, she managed to get a meal together out of the meagre ingredients in the fridge. Her mother had taught her well, as there was never a surplus of money in their household and very little was wasted, particularly when it came to food. She realised that this was the first meal she had cooked in her role as Mrs Owen Brewster and hoped that it would please her husband.

They ate in silence and when finished, Owen laid down his cutlery and said, "That wasn't too bad," which Caroline took to mean it was at least edible. She did notice that there was no "Thanks" attached to the comment. However, his lack of gratitude was not surprising. Thinking back over their relationship, she reasoned that he had never actually been enthusiastic about food but only how much he could save with his vouchers and leaving the pizza place before the full-price menus kicked in.

They checked into the hotel, and as instructed, Caroline mentioned that they were on their honeymoon and they were greeted with an unenthusiastic "That's nice" from the person on the other side of the counter. No upgrade seemed to be forthcoming, or a bottle of bubbly, so Owen decided to see if he could do any better.

"Yes, we only got married yesterday," he announced in a loud voice to the booking clerk. "Any chance of an upgrade or a bottle of champagne?" The booking clerk gave him a straight stare and said, "Sir, you are booked in at a budget rate for one night only. It is not possible to do anything for you, but we hope you enjoy your stay" and handed him the key. Caroline blushed with embarrassment at this exchange and started to tug at Owen's arm to move him away from the counter. "Let's just go, Owen," she pleaded with him. She hated scenes, especially if she was in the middle of them.

There was no one to take their bags to their room, so Owen carried his and handed Caroline hers while they proceeded towards the lifts. The found their room and he was dismayed to find that their windows faced a awfully uninviting view of a construction site. He was very angry and rang the booking desk downstairs. They were sympathetic, as they had been trained to be, but explained that their budget rooms did not offer a view and they would be quite happy to let him have a better room, which of course would be double the cost. Owen didn't even bother to reply before he slammed the phone down.

Well that got the honeymoon off to a great start.

Caroline set about unpacking her suitcase. Actually it wasn't "her" suitcase as such, because she had never been anywhere to need one. It was her mother's and didn't even have wheels like all the modern ones did. Owen's wasn't any newer, and she suspected that his was inherited as well.

Caroline took her clothes into the bathroom, as she wasn't yet comfortable undressing in front of her new husband, and reappeared dressed in slacks and a shirt with sneakers and socks. Owen took one look at her and asked, "Is that the best you can do when we are staying for a night in the city?"

This comment got under Caroline's skin, and she tersely replied, "Well, I can always go out and buy something new while we are here." Buying new clothes at city prices was not high on his spending agenda. "Anyway, you have only got a pair of your suit pants and a shirt on." Owen knew he wasn't winning this battle so just picked up the room key and indicated with a sweep of his hand towards the door that Caroline should precede him into the corridor.

They were in the cheaper end of town so decided to have a walk around and maybe catch a bus down to the waterfront, but Owen pointed out that they wouldn't be eating dinner there but would eat closer to their hotel. The afternoon had apparently been mapped out with no consultation with Caroline. She just tagged along behind him while they walked for what felt like kilometres until they got to the waterfront.

Well, not exactly an island resort or Fiji, but I can at least see the water and all the boats going back and forth. I guess that will have to do.

She was getting hot and thirsty after all the walking so suggested that they get something to drink. He thought she meant alcohol and with a shocked look on his face he said, "It is hardly time for a drink. It is only four-thirty." Caroline reassured him she didn't mean alcohol, just something cold. She was astounded when he came back with a small bottle of water and two straws. "I thought we could share."

After a bit more sightseeing it was time to get the bus back to the other end of town and Owen asked Caroline if she had any change for the fare. She duly handed over the requested amount to the driver, was given their tickets, and they found a seat. She was surprised when they got off a few stops before their hotel, but Owen reassured her that he had found a great place to eat. She was expecting somewhere that had a special for Sunday night, or half-price if out before seven, but what Owen had come up with left her absolutely speechless.

He directed her towards what looked like a shopping mall in Chinatown and when she got near the doorway her nostrils were assailed by smells she had never known before. The noise that emanated from that same doorway was deafening and in a language she didn't understand. Owen had found a food court catering to Asian students where you paid for a bowl and could have as much boiled rice and noodles as you wanted, with a choice of two scoops from the hot food counter.

This was not quite the dining experience that Caroline expected on the night of her honeymoon. However, not wanting to cause a scene, she readily accepted the bowl handed to her by the lady behind the counter who directed with her hands where the rice and noodle bins were located and indicated that she should then come back and choose her two dishes to go on top.

This was a whole new way of eating to Caroline and as the signs on the food were not in English, she was dubious about what the red, brown or cream-coloured dishes actually consisted of. Most of the vegetables she could identify, as there was an Asian grocery store not far from where she had lived, but as far as the rest of it went, she would just have to choose two and hope for the best. With a large scoop of gluey white rice dumped in her bowl by the unsmiling fellow behind the bins, Caroline proceeded to the hot food counter and chose one brown and one cream-coloured scoop.

The challenge now was to find a table to sit at. The place was quite crowded, even though it was Sunday night, but Owen managed to hover around a table until the two people occupying it vacated. Caroline was thinking about the rice going cold in the bottom of the bowl, but even worse the two scoops on top cooling into a gelatinous mess. Well, this was dinner—Owen style, so she might as well try to enjoy it.

Once they were seated, she smiled at Owen and hoped his humour had improved since it had taken them ten minutes to find this miniscule square of Formica-topped and metal-edged table tucked in a corner. The accompanying stools were moulded plastic and very uncomfortable. Perhaps this was a ruse by the owners. Don't make people too comfortable so they stay longer. Get them in and get them out! More turnover equals more money. The whole dining experience for Caroline and Owen took just over thirty minutes, and they were out the door and walking in the direction of their hotel.

It was only seven and she was in no rush to repeat last night's coupling. She was still sore but suspected that Owen would not take rejection very well. After the bathroom routine of "No, you go first" Caroline was settling down to watch television, in the only chair provided in the room, when Owen emerged dressed in the same pyjamas as the night before. He was a little surprised to see Caroline wasn't in bed and suggested that she turn off the TV and "perform your wifely duties." Had she heard right? That was such an archaic way of speaking, but then again, Owen wasn't a 21st century man from what she had observed.

She thought she would make a stand for "wifely independence" and told Owen that she really didn't feel like it tonight. She thought he was going to explode with anger as he paced up and down the room, going on about how he had gotten a poor deal with her and after all the money he had spent on this room and so on. She sighed and just to keep the peace, she picked up the remote and the TV screen went to black. It was a bit how she felt on the inside, on this the second night of her marriage.

She reluctantly got into the empty side of the bed and pulled the quilt up to her shoulders. Owen proceeded with his version of lovemaking, and it was all Caroline could do not to vomit her rice and two scoops all over the pristine bed linen. Her last thought before he launched himself on top of her was *where did he learn all this horrible stuff?*

Breakfast was not part of the deal so Owen had gotten up before Caroline woke and sourced out some fresh sweet rolls from a nearby bakery in Chinatown. He proudly produced them as he came back in the door and announced that they didn't need any butter, as they were quite moist. He handed Caroline her roll in a paper bag and proceeded to bite into his roll.

"I will make us a cup of tea from the teabags here" Owen announced. He found cups but was horrified at the thick white china. "Not the Royal Albert I am used to, but they will have to do". He then proceeded to empty the small tray of every teabag, coffee stick, sugar and biscuits. At the look of amazement on Caroline's face he defended his actions with "Well, if we don't take them home the people who clean the room will steal them. Besides, I have paid for them, they haven't. Here, put them in your handbag." Caroline did as she was commanded.

After their meagre breakfast, Owen sat in the single chair and started to read through the papers he had purchased on his way back from the bakery. Caroline was ignored so, sitting on the bed, took the opportunity to put the television on and see what was happening in the world. Owen dropped the paper just below his eyelevel and gave Caroline a hard stare.

"Do you have to have the television on while I am trying to read the newspaper?"

"Yes, I do" she answered. "You are ignoring me, so what else am I supposed to do?" Owen's silent reply was to put the newspaper back up to it previous level, but not before he gave it a good shake to emphasise his displeasure.

Checkout time was 11 a.m. and Owen wasn't going to leave one minute earlier than he had paid for. He had worked out the train and bus timetables to get them back home and with two minutes to spare until checkout, he folded the paper, put it in his suitcase and enquired of his new wife "Are you ready to leave?" Caroline's silent answer was to pick up her packed suitcase and head for the door.

Day Two of being Mrs Owen Brewster had ended, and it hadn't come soon enough for Caroline.

Chapter 9

Monday afternoon was spent generally cleaning the house. Very quietly Caroline relocated the offending apron from behind the door to the back of a cupboard. She couldn't believe it when Owen appeared in the kitchen a few minutes later and asked her "Where has my mother's apron gone?" Caroline knew she couldn't pretend she didn't know, so decided to bluff it out. "It doesn't fit me and it is all faded so I am going to wash it." Her reply must have satisfied Owen but he didn't work out that aprons are fairly much 'one size fits all'. If Caroline had anything to do with it, this apron would fall apart in the wash and have to be consigned to the rubbish bin.

Tuesday morning arrived and they both got ready to return to work. They still needed to establish a bathroom routine as they seemed to be getting in each other's way but eventually, and a little late, they arrived at work.

They were greeted with smirks from a few of their workmates and overheard a few ribald remarks that they chose to ignore, albeit with red faces, as they headed to their respective cubbyholes they called offices. Caroline's boss enquired, "So how did it go?"

"It was very nice thanks." Her boss had meant the sexual side of things and Caroline meant the wedding. Her boss thought that Owen wouldn't be a very good lover because he was so selfish, and she didn't know how right she was.

The talk around the water cooler that Tuesday morning seemed a bit more ribald than normal to Caroline's ears and she suspected that they were having a go at her and Owen, but she wasn't brave enough to challenge them. Well, they could say what they liked as far as she was concerned. It was her life and none of their business what happened between her sheets. She certainly wasn't going to enlighten them about how disappointed she was in the whole subject of marriage and the marital bed in particular.

It seemed strange when she and Owen were travelling home from work together. They found a seat and Owen proceeded to open a newspaper that he had found in the park when he went to lunch. When Caroline looked sideways, it was all that she could do to not burst out laughing. The 'free' paper was in Italian and to her knowledge Owen knew no foreign languages.

What some people will do to appear better educated than they are.

She had very few of her own possessions and hadn't yet been able to bring Hurry's ashes to her new address. That was one thing she would have her way on, even if it meant hiding them somewhere. Her only successful act of defiance had been the red kettle and toaster sitting on the bench in the kitchen. Owen had refused to use either appliance as he thought they were cheap and tacky and continued filling the old kettle that sat on the gas stove and made a loud whistle when the water was hot enough. He would have had a fit if he knew how much they had actually cost, but she wasn't about to tell him or they would have gone on eBay like her beautiful queen-size mattress.

Owen made it quite clear that he did not intend to eat his dinner from plates balanced on rattan place mats like the natives use. Where he got that bit of information was anybody's guess but he needed to have an opinion. He wanted the whole embroidered cloth scene and so the table was set each meal with linen serviettes (paper ones were a waste of money), but he did allow Caroline to use their ugly wedding gift dinner set. Caroline didn't really care about the cloth and serviettes until Owen made it clear he expected them, each weekend, to be hand washed and starched (who even knew how to starch linen anymore?) before being pressed and ready for the next week.

Caroline hadn't had the need to venture out to the laundry, and when she did she stopped in her tracks. It was in its original condition! Cement floor; cement washing tub, and a little twin-tub washing machine that looked as though two pairs of socks would fill it up. She didn't have a clue how to work the thing, but obviously Owen would because he had lived here all his life. He was quite happy to give her instructions about how to put the household laundry through it, but insisted that his white shirts be washed by hand and hung on hangers so they would last longer. His five ties—no, six since his wedding tie had been added to the collection—should also have the same treatment. She didn't enquire what he expected her to do with his socks and jocks as she suspected she wouldn't like the answer.

When they had been married one week Owen instructed that they would be going to the storage unit to empty it out and bring "home" what she needed and throw the rest out. Caroline said that she would rather go alone, and this idea was not received very well, but she stood her ground. What was in the storage unit was hers, and she would deal with it how she saw fit, she informed Owen. She didn't want him to see where she was going to hide Hurry's ashes and the boxes of memorabilia her mother had saved over almost three decades. At least none of the aforementioned would have brought any money on eBay, she thought, so they were probably safe, but she wasn't 100% sure on that.

She drove Betty to the storage place. Over the previous few weeks she had been saving boxes from her supermarket shopping to pack the last of her belongings in. She had already pared them down when she left her parents' house and then again when she moved into the home unit, but there was still more than she thought Owen would be happy with integrating into the household. Most of the cupboards were full of his mother's cooking equipment, linen, see-through thin bath towels and family photo albums. She too had some linen from her mother, which was actually nicer than what she put on the table each night, and thought it might be a welcome addition to the décor. She was definitely going to find her thick white fluffy towel with *Caroline* embroidered on it.

Betty was packed with boxes and the keys handed back to the storage manager. They would send her a cheque to cover the unused weeks. She gave them her new name and address and drove out of the driveway headed for "home." She was having a lot of trouble thinking of it as her home but maybe when she had a few more of her belongings around she would feel differently. She certainly hoped so because she was going to be very unhappy if she couldn't get over this hurdle.

Owen helped her carry some of the boxes inside and wanted to know if there was anything that needed to go to the tip or could be sold. She frostily answered, "No thanks, it is all staying here. We will just have to make room for it in the cupboards." He shrugged his shoulders, made no more comment, and gave her no help from that point on. Caroline continued to make trip after trip from Betty to the house and after about an hour had all the boxes stacked in the lounge room.

Owen was conspicuous by his absence and she wondered where he had gone. She looked out the window and was surprised to see him washing her car and then cleaning the inside. *That's most unusual, I usually do that. Oh well, maybe he is just trying to make up for being mean. I will make him a nice cup of tea when he is finished, and I will use those detested cups.*

An hour had gone by, and Owen hadn't returned to the house. Caroline looked out the window, and Betty was nowhere to be seen. "Perhaps he has gone to check the tyres," she said to herself. Another hour went by, and finally she saw Owen walking up the road. Walking? What had happened to Betty? Maybe he had had an accident, but he didn't look injured. She opened the front door and asked, "Where have you been?" She didn't recognise the look on his face but it was somewhere between evil and triumph.

"I sold Betty," he replied as he pushed past her.

"You did what?" yelled Caroline.

"Are you deaf as well as stupid? I sold Betty."

"But you couldn't. I bought her in my name." By this time Caroline was feeling that she didn't really know much about this man she had married a week ago.

"Your signature is not that difficult" was his reply as he grinned and walked past her, waving a cheque under her nose. "This will boost our bank account nicely."

Caroline just looked at him with tears in her eyes. Her beloved Betty, her bit of freedom, had been sold, and she had no way of getting her back.

When, in her pre-wedded ignorance, they had set up a bank account in both their names, it escaped her notice that any cheques had to have both signatures. Owen wasn't prepared to use a plastic card in an ATM and without a card her money was locked away. She had never shared a bank account with anyone and was therefore unaware of the pit she had just dug for herself. Caroline was instructed "sign here, and here". Owen had included Caroline's savings and bank deposit into their joint account but had kept his own money separate. Her financial freedom had gone without her even being aware of it. Owen was fully in control of their shared assets: the money from the sale of her parent's house, the cheque for Betty, and any other money that went into that account, including her weekly pay.

He was triumphant, and she was devastated. He knew how much she earned at work; however, she wasn't privy to that information about him. All her money was in an account that she had access to but only if Owen was a co-signatory on a cheque, and she had no plastic card that she could use for withdrawals. She knew she had been tricked and felt trapped!

Caroline spent Sunday opening the boxes she had liberated from the storage unit and trying to find places to store the contents. Owen had reluctantly cleared his mother's clothes out of the wardrobe he indicated Caroline could use. She left the doors open for a few days because the interior smelt of mothballs, and she didn't want her few clothes to take on that aroma.

She found Hurry's small box of ashes and put them at the back of her underwear drawer. Some of the boxes of memorabilia from her mother were carefully put in the wardrobe behind the few jumpers she had stored on a top shelf. The remaining ones she pushed in behind her longer coats and dresses but fortunately Owen wasn't aware of their existence so it was unlikely he would go looking for them.

He had decided to take the weekend papers out into the sun and read them from cover to cover. The Sunday papers were one of his very rare indulgences but as he would tell anyone who cared to listen, and there were few enough of those, he liked to keep up with what was going on in the world. He would read the financial section from front to back and felt that it made him very well informed for any decisions he needed to make at work.

Caroline was aware that nobody at work asked for his opinion on anything—financial or otherwise. His colleagues considered him to be just a paper shuffler of a very low rank, sitting in a brown suit, in a corner somewhere. His function was to do all the jobs nobody else wanted, or could be bothered to do, such as balancing the petty cash. This was usually incorrect because people didn't always put dockets in for purchases. There were vouchers with descriptions and amounts that didn't match and Owen laboured for hours to get this exactly right. When he managed to achieve this, he would send an internal email around to inform everyone that the petty cash for this month had balanced. He was the office joke, but he was so full of his own importance that he didn't realise it.

Caroline prepared a hot meal for lunch, as decreed by Owen, because then they would have some cold meat for their lunches on Monday. They sat on opposite sides of the table, and it was a few minutes before Owen noticed." What's that?" he enquired, pointing to the tablecloth.

"It's one of Mum's cloths. I thought it would make a nice change," explained Caroline.

"If I want anything changed, I will let you know. I don't want to see it again," Owen told his new wife.

Caroline just sat there with a stunned look on her face. She continued her meal in silence and when finished got up from the table, washed up, and removed the offending cloth. She took it into their bedroom and secreted it in her wardrobe. She was beginning to realise that she knew less and less about this man she had married and really didn't like what she did know.

She lay down on the top of the quilt covering their double bed and didn't even bother to remove her shoes. She was miserable and was becoming very wary of Owen's reaction to the most mundane domestic issues. What did it matter which cloth was on the table? He had managed to get her to put away those "native" place mats that used to look quite smart on Caroline's glass table in her other life, as she thought of it. Now he didn't want her mother's cloth on the table.

What else is he capable of?

She started to think about how her life had changed in the last three months, and certainly not for the better. Owen liked to be in control; that much was evident by the bank account issue and selling Betty. How could she carve out a bit of independence for herself without getting a backlash from him? He knew how much she earned, so putting some of that in another bank account wasn't an option. He handed her money each week for the housekeeping and as she had to keep the dockets for everything, much like the petty cash at work, she couldn't put any money aside from that.

From the recesses of her mind she remembered that she still had to get the balance of the storage unit money back. It was only a few hundred dollars, but it would be a start. She would ring them tomorrow and ask if they could send the cheque to work rather than home as Owen collected all the mail every evening from the post box and went through it thoroughly. He paid all the bills on time so as not to incur a late fee and posted them from work using company envelopes and stamps.

Her cheque arrived at work and she asked her boss how she could turn it into cash. Her boss was absolutely amazed that this twenty-eight-year-old and intelligent young woman had been coerced into opening a bank account over which she had no control. She suggested that she would phone the company cashier, a friend, and arrange for Caroline to cash her cheque. Caroline was delighted and made a vow to herself that this money would be hers not "theirs."

Chapter 10
Margie

Margie was in love with life, even though life had not always been in love with Margie. She had married Ron, her high school sweetheart, when she was just twenty-one years old, and they had all the hopes and dreams that most people their age did.

She was no beauty, but everyone who spoke about her said she was a beautiful person. Her curly blond hair was invariably piled on top of her head as it was too unruly to leave loose and she had the bluest eyes, edged by long black lashes. Her skin was smooth and her rosy cheeks gave her a look of glowing health. According to women's magazines she was a little overweight, but it was evenly distributed and gave her a curvy look that was much admired by the boys who were always trying to give her a cuddle.

Margie wasn't a flirt, and she just gave them a gentle push away with a smile, warning, "I will send Ron after you" and the boys just laughed and went on their way. It was well known that Ron and Margie were "a couple" and had been for most of high school. Ron was the perfect foil for Margie's blond looks, as he was slightly taller than her, with dark hair and eyes. His skin tanned easily in the summer sun as he spent most of his spare time outdoors.

Ron was just two years older and didn't plan to go on to college. He wanted to take up an apprenticeship and work in a mechanical area. He loved tinkering with anything that resembled an engine and as a child had pulled things apart and put them back together, rarely with any bits left over.

Ron and Margie always knew they would be together, and after their marriage they took out a lease on a small flat which they furnished with whatever they could afford or refurbish to make their home comfortable. They planned to wait a few years to have a family so that Ron could establish himself in the world of business. They would buy a lovely home in which to raise their children and would become the sought-after "two parents two children two cars" family. However, the gods conspired against them.

When he had finished his apprenticeship, and borrowed money from the bank where he had regularly deposited some part of his pocket money, Ron established a small mechanical workshop with the hope that he could build up the business into a profit-making enterprise. Margie, in the meantime, was working as a part-time waitress in a coffee shop. It wasn't too physically taxing for her but helped Ron's rather low income from the business and every week they each put some money away for their future together.

It was essential to her that she was home to prepare their evening meal and have time to look after the domestic side of things. In her mind, and Ron's too, this job of hers was only until they started their family. When Margie first suspected she was pregnant, and a chemist bought test proved she was right, she and Ron were overjoyed. Margie went to her own doctor the next day to confirm the good news. They had begun their family and couldn't wait for their son or daughter to make its way into their world.

Margie immediately gave notice at the coffee shop, even though she was only six weeks pregnant, because she had a very strong nesting instinct and wanted to start preparing the nursery for their first child. With time on her hands, she spent hours in the baby section of every store she could find, picking up little clothes and gently handling beautiful bedding. A lot of her day was spent daydreaming about what he or she would like; would he or she look like her or Ron? What would the baby's personality be like? Would he or she be a happy, contented child, as they grew older?

Then the awful day came when she was ten weeks pregnant that Margie felt cramping pain in her lower abdomen, and it momentarily took her breath away. She was doubled over and another young woman coming out of the store behind her stopped and put her hand on Margie's shoulder. "Are you okay?" she asked with a worried look on her face. Margie couldn't even answer her; she just shook her head with tears in her eyes. "I need to get to my doctor. I think I am miscarrying," she finally gasped out in between sharp intakes of breath.

The young woman offered to take her in her car and Margie was very grateful. "My name is Rebecca," she volunteered. Margie could just nod at Rebecca as she was in so much pain. It was all that Margie could manage to direct Rebecca to her doctor's address. She finally gasped, "Could you call my husband for me and ask him to meet me at our doctor's?" and Rebecca replied that of course she would. She wrote her own number down on a piece of paper and put it in the top of Margie's bag.

She had liked Margie on first sight and wanted to keep in touch if that was at all possible. She was booked to go on a holiday to Spain the next day but hoped to contact Margie when she got back to see how she was.

When they reached the doctor's surgery, just one look by the receptionist at Margie's face told her all she needed to know and she quickly ushered her into an empty surgery and buzzed the doctor who was in with another patient. "We have an emergency," she whispered into the phone. "I think Margie is miscarrying. She is in room 4." The doctor excused himself from his consultation and quickly went in to see what, if anything, he could do for Margie, who was one of his favourite patients.

He briefly examined Margie and then asked the receptionist to ring an ambulance. He held her hand gently and told her that she was miscarrying and would need to go to hospital. Margie burst into tears. "What did I do wrong, doctor?"

"Nothing, Margie, it is just the way some pregnancies go at around ten to twelve weeks. You did nothing to cause it nor could you have stopped it happening. I am so sorry, Margie."

Just as the ambulance arrived in the surgery driveway, Ron pulled up beside it and leaving the door open and the engine running ran into the doctor's. He went into the room indicated by the receptionist and was shocked to see Margie. She had tears running down her face and was very pale as she lay on the bed with blood on her clothes.

"She will have to go to hospital, Ron. She is miscarrying, and I am so sorry for you both. Go in the ambulance with her, and I will arrange for my secretary to park your car, and you can pick it up later."

Ron put his arms around Margie and whispered in her ear, "It's alright, darling. It's not your fault and I am here for you as I always will be." Margie gave him a rather watery smile and a little wave as the paramedics wheeled her down the corridor and placed her gently in the ambulance.

"You can get in the back with your wife if you want to," one of the paramedics said to Ron, but he already had his foot on the bottom step. They weren't leaving him behind while his wife went through this ordeal.

He loved Margie so much and his heart ached for her. They had both been so looking forward to this new addition to their life, but it had been cruelly snatched away from them. He thought that when she was back on her feet again and feeling well, they could try for another baby and hope that this one would go full term. Ron spent a couple of anxious hours in the corridor outside the operating theatre where they had taken Margie "to tidy her up," as one of the nurses put it. Ron didn't even have time to ask her what that meant before he was left alone sitting on a hard vinyl chair, staring at the opposite wall.

He knew he should ring his parents and Margie's too, but he just didn't have the heart at the moment. When he was sure that she was okay, they would do that together. His darling wife was his first priority. When Margie came out of the theatre and she was put in a ward, she looked pale and he was very worried about her. The attending nurse assured him that she was okay; she had lost a bit of blood, but as she was a healthy young woman she would recover fairly quickly. Ron sat with Margie and was horrified when her first words to him were "I am so sorry."

He slipped his arms under her shoulders and with his head next to hers on the pillow he whispered, "It was not your fault, darling. You did nothing wrong. It is sometimes just nature's way, and we can try again later when you are well. We will be a family but just a little later than we planned." Margie's eyes filled up with tears, and she just nodded her head.

Ron arranged with a friend later that day to help him collect his car. He went from there straight to the hospital to get Margie and drive her home. After all the discharge papers were signed and Margie had a list of instructions in her hand, she noticed that there was a card pinned to the top which was for a support service after losing a child. She wasn't ready to go to group therapy or whatever they did, but she tucked it away in her bag anyway.

When they arrived at their front door, Ron helped Margie as she slowly made her way into the kitchen. As she passed the door to the nursery she burst into tears and was inconsolable for a few minutes while she wept her grief into his shoulder. She just wanted to go to bed and put the whole awful experience behind her until she felt well enough to maybe try again. At the moment she couldn't imagine when that might be.

Ron gently helped her get ready for bed and tucked the sheets and quilt around her. He couldn't come to grips with the idea that the last time Margie was in this bed was yesterday morning when he kissed her gently on the forehead before he went to work. She had looked so relaxed and happy, unlike the woman he was looking down on now. He didn't know what to say to her, or what to do, so he kissed her on the forehead, told her he loved her, and went out of the room.

He was bewildered. How had this happened and how much heartache could one heart take? If he felt this bad, how must Margie feel when she had been the one carrying this child? He had never been close to his father and mother so felt he couldn't really talk to them about this awful thing that had happened to him and his wife. He had no close friends at work that would even begin to understand the ache where his heart should be.

He dialled his parents' number and his mother answered with her usual cheery "Hello."

"Mum, it's Ron. I just wanted to let you know that Margie miscarried yesterday, but she is okay."

"Oh Ron, how awful for you both. But never mind, you are both young and can try again. It is not the end of the world, and it wasn't yet a baby anyway, was it really?"

Ron could not believe what he was hearing, but then he shouldn't have been surprised because his mother didn't like what she would call "unpleasant situations." She had always found it hard to deal with emotional issues and it was obvious she hadn't gained any life skills on that score in the last decade.

"Well anyway, I just wanted to let you know. Have to go now to check on Margie. Talk to you later. Let Dad know, will you?" He collapsed into the closest chair and closed his eyes in despair. He would have to get a brave mask going before he could face his wife. She could read him like a book and would know that he was upset and it wouldn't do for both of them to fall into a heap. He had to be the strong one in this situation.

He quietly opened the bedroom door to see if Margie was awake. She was lying on her side with her back to him, but he could see her shoulders shaking while she quietly sobbed into the pillow. He couldn't bear to see her like this so closed the door and went into the kitchen to make a cup of coffee. He sat with the coffee, untouched, until it went cold and then threw it down the sink. His thoughts were in a whirl.

He knew Margie needed him, and he needed her, but he was afraid of breaking down in front of her and seeming weak so he stayed away from her for the next few hours. When he next opened the bedroom door, she was lying on her back just staring up at the ceiling. She turned her tear-stained face towards him, and he gulped back his tears. "Would you like something to eat or drink?" She just shook her head. He couldn't believe the change in his wife in just twenty-four hours. He asked her if she would like her mother to come and stay with her, but she just shook her head again.

"I just want to rest," she replied. Ron reached over, squeezed Margie's hand, and walked from the room with sadness in his eyes. He was at an absolute loss to know what to do for her.

Days went by and Margie was still in bed when Ron left to go to work and was there again when he returned. She had been in the same nightwear for days, her hair unkempt and her face tear stained. He gently tried coaxing her to get up and have a shower, put on some clean clothes, but she didn't seem to have the energy or, even more worrying to Ron, the *will* to get back into living.

Ron decided he would go and visit their family doctor who had attended to Margie when she miscarried. He didn't know if he could help him much, but he had to talk to someone or he felt he would go mad. It was no use trying to talk to his parents as his mother just trotted out the usual platitudes of "it's not the end of the world," etc. He was storing all his fear and anxiety inside but on the outside looked as though he was his normal self. He was so afraid of crying in front of someone at work, or in the street, and making a fool of himself.

Chapter 11

Two weeks after her miscarriage, Margie was starting to feel a bit more like her old self, although she was still so incredibly sad. She had told her mother what had happened but had received a similar response to what Ron had from his mother. Was there no one who could understand how she was feeling? Then she remembered the card for the support group that had been attached to her discharge papers. Maybe someone who had been in her position would understand what she was feeling—the grief, the hopelessness, the smashing of their dreams for a family.

The doctors at the hospital had told her that physically she could bear another child, but she didn't know if emotionally she would cope, especially if the same thing happened again. The doctor had reassured her that there was no reason to believe that she would suffer another miscarriage, but then again he couldn't guarantee that she wouldn't either.

While she was trying to find the card, she noticed a piece of paper with Rebecca's name and phone number on it. Margie felt that she and Rebecca could be friends and also she wanted to thank her for her help on that dreadful day. She didn't want to think about how she would have managed to get help if Rebecca hadn't stopped and enquired if she was okay. She saw the postscript that said she was booked on a holiday to Spain, leaving the day after they had met, but maybe they could catch up when she got back in a few weeks.

Margie thought Rebecca would probably be back from Spain by now and she would try to contact her within the next few days. When Margie rang the number for the support group she spoke to a lovely young woman, Jeannie, who reassured her that they could try to help her get through this awful time. She arranged to meet Jeannie the next Tuesday night at a local hall and she would be introduced to the others in the group. It struck Margie that she was no longer alone and other young women had suffered the same experience that she had. This lightened her mood, and she felt strong enough to go and buy some special food for their dinner that night.

As soon as Ron opened the door he noticed the change. Margie was looking more like the wife he had had a few weeks ago. She walked into his open arms, and as they embraced he told her, "I have missed you, my darling." They hugged as though they would never let go but finally broke away from each other and Margie announced that she had cooked a special dinner for them.

Over dinner she told Ron about the support group she had contacted and that she would be meeting Jeannie on Tuesday night. He was very glad that she had taken this step, because although he loved her so much it sometimes hurt—he had no more to give and what he had given was not enough. He wasn't a female so he couldn't know what it felt like to be carrying a child and to have it cruelly ripped from you, even though it had been smaller than the palm of his hand.

Margie also mentioned her mother's response, which was so similar to her mother-in-law's platitudes that it was almost as though the two women had read the same script. A miscarriage had never happened to either of them, as far as she knew, so they would have no idea what it felt like, but a bit of empathy would have gone a long way.

Tuesday night arrived and Ron drove her to the local hall for her seven o'clock meeting with Jeannie who was waiting outside to meet her. As Margie emerged from the car she couldn't help but notice the number of other young women who were chatting and walking towards the light from within the rectangle of the doorway, and this gave her immediate comfort.

She kissed Ron goodbye and arranged for him to pick her up after the meeting, coffee, and biscuits at ten. Jeannie was of slight build, with long blond hair and the lithesome walk of a ballerina. Margie was introduced to the ten other women, and they all welcomed her with a smile. Nametags were handed out, which was a ritual especially when a new member came along, and Margie was shown to a seat in the circle. The chairs were all as different as the women sitting on them, and Margie felt that she belonged, even though she had only been there for less than ten minutes.

The group were asked who would like to speak and one young woman with a halo of dark curly hair stood up. "Hi, my name is Sara, and I had a stillborn little girl one year ago today. Happy birthday, Samantha." And then she sat back down. Almost with one movement the other women rose from their chairs and went to stand with Sara to wait their turn to give her a supportive hug.

Some of the women chose not to speak but just told the group, "Not today, thanks."

When it was Margie's turn she just stood up and said, "I had a miscarriage about a month ago, and I am not coping. I can't seem to get up in the morning and feel that I have lost my way. My husband means well, but he isn't coping either, and I am afraid that I am losing him as well."

One by one, those who wanted to spoke about their experiences and how people assumed that because the pregnancy didn't go full term it wasn't a real baby. Friends made comments such as "You can try again. You are only young," but they didn't understand the fear behind trying again and perhaps having the same result.

One young woman by the name of Hope said that her name was by no means an indication of how she was feeling. The group laughed at that as Hope had a great sense of humour, but she struggled with her loss as much as any of them. She told Margie that she tried to shrug off comments of well-meaning friends with a humorous comeback, but underneath it hurt like a dagger in her ribs. One of the worst things to be endured were comments like "at least you never got fat like a bowling ball" or "you got your figure back quickly because you weren't very big." Hope made the comment that the media had a lot to answer for with this obsession about getting your pre-baby body back. It was assumed that all women had the body of a goddess before they even became pregnant. A lot of the group laughed at this and one piped up with the comment "We wish".

After the meeting part of the evening, the girls adjourned to a place at the back of the hall where coffee had been set up, and someone had brought a chocolate cake, as it was her turn to provide the food. It looked absolutely beautiful and was devoured within minutes. As they left the hall, Jeannie asked her if she was okay about the meeting and would she come again? Margie told her, "It was just what I needed and I will be here in two weeks for the next one." Jeannie was delighted, and as Ron pulled up in the car, Margie beckoned him over to be introduced to her new friend.

When they arrived home he asked her how she felt about going to the meeting and what had they talked about? She explained how supportive they all were and about Sara's little girl who had been stillborn one year ago today. Ron listened to Margie while she opened up and told him most of what had gone on, and he couldn't help but notice how much more relaxed she was. It was the first time he had seen her smile since the day they had lost their baby.

Ron made the comment that he thought he could do with a group like that, and it was then Margie had a "light bulb moment." She turned to Ron and said, "Well, why don't you start one? Men are not renowned for their communication at times like this, but just one meeting has helped me such a lot." Ron said that he would consider it, and he looked thoughtful as he went into the kitchen to pour himself a drink. He asked Margie if she would like a wine, and they took their glasses outside to their favourite spot in the garden.

While they had their drinks they bounced ideas off each other about how they would get the men's group off the ground, where they would hold it and how often. Ron decided to go and see if their family doctor could help with putting him in touch with men who had suffered a similar tragedy. Patient confidentiality did not allow the doctor to give Ron this information, but he did offer to put up a notice in the waiting room. He also suggested that Ron have cards printed, similar to the one that Margie had received, and he would pass them on.

Margie felt that it would be good for Ron to do this as he was struggling almost as much as she was, but now she had found a group of women who understood what she had gone through and was still going through. She felt that her healing could begin and she could look forward to the future, whatever it held for them as a couple. They went to bed that night and made love for the first time since their baby had been lost, and it was wonderful for both of them. A bridge back to each other had been crossed.

Chapter 12

Another month went by, and Margie felt that she had emerged from a fog, an inertia that had kept her tethered to the house and without any joy in her heart. She had been to two more meetings and when she opened her address book to ring Jeannie from the support group, the piece of paper with Rebecca's number fell out and fluttered to the floor. Margie felt more able now to contact the young woman who had been a stranger then, but had helped her when she had needed it.

Rebecca answered the phone very quickly and was rather breathless. "Hi, Rebecca, it's Margie here, the woman you helped to the doctor's. Sorry it has taken me so long to get in touch with you. How was Spain?"

Rebecca was so pleased to hear from Margie, and after a bit of chatter, they arranged to meet up for coffee. She said she would tell Margie all about her holiday then. At ten o'clock the next day the two new friends met and hugged as though they had known each other for years.

They were completely different in looks; Margie was blonde and curvy whereas Rebecca was tall, slim and had dark curly hair down to her shoulders. She still sported her holiday tan and was wearing a long loose dress printed in orange and purple. When they were seated in the coffee shop and had ordered their food and drinks, Rebecca asked, "How are you feeling?"

Margie told her how miserable she had been and how much better she felt since joining the support group. She also told her about Ron researching starting up a group for men who had gone through the same experience he had.

"Now, tell me about Spain. Did you have a good time? Did you meet anyone?" Rebecca leaned back in her chair and proceeded to regale Margie with hilarious stories of the places she had seen, the strange people she had met on the day tours in Spain, and left the best part for last.

"I met this gorgeous man, Luis," Rebecca began. "We went out a few times to local places to eat and drink, but I don't think the Spanish wine agreed with me. I got drunk so quickly that I am not sure what happened most of the time."

"Was Luis on the tour?" Margie enquired.

"No, he ran a local tour company and of course all the ladies liked him, but he chose me as his date for those few outings. I am sure it is against company policy, but he is the boss so I guess he could change the rules." Rebecca then went quiet, and Margie said, "Are you okay? You look a bit pale, even under your suntan."

"Margie, you know how some people bring home fridge magnets from their holidays?"

"Yes."

"Well, I brought home a baby."

Margie's eyes opened wider and, until she really looked at Rebecca's face, she thought she must have been joking. "Oh, Rebecca, what are you going to do?"

Rebecca's eyes welled with tears and she lowered her head. "I don't know, Margie. I really don't know. I have a job, but my employment won't be for long once they find out I am single and pregnant to a man I will probably never see again."

"Will you have an abortion, keep the baby, or have it adopted out?" Margie asked.

"I am against abortion for many reasons, and I would really like to keep the baby if I could find a way to do so. I don't think I could cope with going through a pregnancy, giving birth and then give up my baby for adoption" Rebecca suddenly realised that Margie hadn't had the opportunity to give birth and added, "I am so sorry, Margie, that was thoughtless of me." But Margie just held her friend's hand and gently squeezed it.

"You were there for me the day I needed you, and I will be here for you whenever you need me, no matter what you decide. Our paths were meant to cross for some reason, and we may never know why, but let's not waste what we have been given."

"Have you told your mother yet?" asked Margie. Rebecca's eyes welled up with tears and she replied in a quiet voice "Yes, and she hung up the phone without saying goodbye. All I got was a lecture on how stupid I had been, that I was always trouble and look where it had gotten me and the comment 'You'd think you would know about birth control at your age.' Her parting words were 'And don't think you are going to come home and cause me disgrace with my Church group either. You have made your bed and now you can go lie in it.'"

"Oh, Rebecca, she is going to be a grandma. Does she realise that?"

"She probably will later, but at the moment all she is concerned about is how me being pregnant is going to impact on her reputation. I should have known better than to expect any support from Mum. She gave Dad a hell of a time when he was alive and was always worried about what other people thought."

There was no point in her trying to contact Luis as he was half a world away and was really only a holiday fling. Rebecca felt that he would not be interested in being a father as every busload that he took on tour probably provided him with a female who thought he was wonderful – much as Rebecca had.

Her pregnancy progressed and she was absolutely glowing. Margie introduced her to her own doctor for her pre-natal visits. She was immediately accepted as a new patient as well as being Margie's saviour on the day of her miscarriage. On those days, the two girls met for coffee as wine was off the drinks list now Rebecca was pregnant. She was very conscious of her diet and doing the best she could for her unborn child. She knew how hard it must be for Margie to see her growing belly.

She had managed to wear loose tops and pants to hide her growing bulge, but by the time she was five months pregnant her situation could no longer be hidden. When the company became aware of her impending motherhood, they asked her to leave. According to management, it gave the customers a bad impression that they would employ someone of dubious morals; single and pregnant.

She had planned to stay a little longer at work as she needed to save some money for the baby's equipment. Fortunately, this archaic way of thinking about pregnant women in the workforce, the law would in future change, especially for single employees.

She was sure her mother wasn't going to help because it might mean being caught out by one of her church friends while she was shopping in the baby section. An explanation of "whose baby?" would be more than her mother could cope with and still keep her head held high within her group of friends. Their opinions mattered more to her than anything else in her small world.

Rebecca was asked to leave work at the end of the week, to keep her hours worked neat and tidy, according to management. Her friends at the company had put in money to buy her some baby goods, but there was nothing forthcoming from the organisation. Obviously they didn't want to show support to an employee who couldn't keep herself virginal. She was very grateful to her workmates because she hadn't managed to buy much herself and only had four months left before her baby was due to be born.

As she carried the basket, balloons, and her handbag up the stairs to her rented unit, her landlady Joyce spied her and came out to the landing."What's the celebration?" she asked in her no-nonsense voice. Rebecca's "nosy-landlady radar" was not working at that particular moment and she replied, "Gifts for my baby."

"But you're not married, and you haven't got a boyfriend," stammered Joyce. She was still asking questions as Rebecca closed her apartment door behind her.

Joyce was determined that she would have the upper hand so, later that night after she had recovered from her shock, she knocked on Rebecca's door. In the next few minutes Joyce made it quite clear to her that she was no longer welcome in her respectable establishment and she could move out at the end of the week.

Rebecca was stunned. She had been a good tenant, quiet, minded her own business, and paid her rent on time. No noisy parties, drugs, or any other unsocial behaviour had caused Joyce problems. Rebecca was now very worried about where she could go with a baby due in less than four months and without an income. Her options were somewhat limited.

As soon as Margie heard about Rebecca's dilemma, she immediately suggested she come and stay with her and Ron until she got herself sorted out. Rebecca was very grateful to her for the immediate solution, but she was worried about how Ron would react and mentioned her concerns.

"Oh, he'll be alright," replied Margie, "but to make you happy I will talk to him about it. We have heaps of room, and Ron is not home all day. I only work part time so you will have the house to yourself during the day. It will be fine." Rebecca went to bed that night very grateful that Margie had come into her life.

Margie and Ron talked for some time over a few glasses of wine. Ron was concerned about how Margie would cope with a baby in the house that was not hers.

"Darling, I am worried about how you will feel when a new baby comes home and is in the nursery where ours should have been".

Margie reassured Ron that she had thought about this exact situation and had decided that 'their' nursery was off-limits. There was a guest room at the back of the house with an adjoining en suite and was quite big enough for Rebecca and some baby equipment. There was even room for a small sofa and a television, so apart from the kitchen, Rebecca and Baby would be self-contained.

"If at any time you are not happy with this arrangement, or if it causes you any emotional stress at all, I want you to tell me and we will work something out. Agreed?" asked Ron, his face full of concern for his beloved wife.

"I promise that I will let you know if that happens" Margie reassured him. She put her arms around Ron and hoped that everything would work out okay. She knew that seeing Rebecca with a new baby would be a mixture of sadness and joy, but she would do the best she could for her wonderful friend.

Rebecca moved out on Saturday and took her meagre belongings to Margie's house, transported in a van that Ron had borrowed. Margie had coffee ready for them all and then helped her put her clothes away. Rebecca left the baby things in the van to bring in later. She had even brought the now-deflating balloons with her as they had been given by friends at work who had been very supportive when they found out she was pregnant.

It was good for Rebecca to be able to talk to Ron without Margie present, as there were a few issues she wanted to clear up. She was worried about how Margie would react to her being pregnant and hopefully delivering a baby when Margie had not been able to do that. Ron assured her that they had discussed just this situation at length and Margie was doing okay and still going to her support group. She seemed to be improving by the month and was almost back to her old self.

"Thank you Rebecca for being so mindful of Margie's situation. You are so good for her but she has promised me that if ever she feels that she can't cope emotionally, she will tell me and we will work something out. In the meantime you are more than welcome to share our home."

Rebecca leaned over and gave Ron a friendly peck on the cheek.

"Thank you Ron, you have no idea how much this means to me. I am glad you and Margie have spoken about the possibility of her being upset. That is the last thing I would want to happen. She has been such a good friend to me and I would not hurt her for anything in the world. Now, I had better concentrate on this unpacking."

Chapter 13

The two women had discussed who would do what around the house to help each other out and the chores were divided equitably. Margie only asked Rebecca to put in for food and help with the power bills. Over the time they had known each other they had become such good friends that they could almost finish each other's sentences. At times Ron felt a bit left out, but he was busy getting his men's group going, and it was proving to be quite a success.

Men are not known for their great communication skills, so with the GP's help, Ron had organised to get a speaker for each meeting and this got things off to a good start. The group were more about having somewhere to go, someone to listen to on a subject they understood, and then being able to have a chat afterwards with others in a similar situation. It was quite a small group at first, only three members who were the partners or husbands of women in Margie's group. The local paper asked Ron if they could come and do an article to help swell the ranks. It was sad for him to think that the members would increase, but that was the hand life dealt you sometimes.

As her due date got closer, Rebecca was more than ever determined to keep her baby. She wasn't sure exactly how she was going to manage money-wise, but her father had left her a small inheritance that remained untouched in the bank that he'd said was "for emergencies" and Rebecca thought that an unmarried mother with no job definitely qualified on that score. Margie had helped her search through the charity shops for what a new baby needed because with so little money there would be no department store shopping for Rebecca. There had been no contact from her mother, so Rebecca made a short phone call to let her know her new address. The information was accepted with no apparent emotion being transmitted down the phone line to her pregnant daughter.

Before Rebecca moved in, Margie had closed the nursery door and not been in there again—out of sight, out of mind. She had days where she had been shopping with Rebecca and pleaded a headache so she could lie on her bed and give in to the tears. She didn't want her friend to know that the sight of her growing belly brought on feelings of melancholy and sometimes she wished she didn't have to look at her. When this happened Margie spoke to one of the girls from her support group about her feelings and sometimes again at the next meeting, which helped her enormously. She needed to get it out of her system, and she knew these recently gained friends understood her pain.

Margie was sound asleep one night when she was woken by Rebecca whispering in her ear, "The baby is coming. I need to go to the hospital. Can you take me?" Margie was up and dressed in a minute and rang the hospital to let them know they were on their way and would be there in about ten minutes. She woke Ron and let him know what was happening and in his sleepy state he just nodded and went back to sleep. *Typical of Ron. He could sleep through anything.*

Ten minutes later Margie pulled up to the Emergency entrance and a stretcher and two attendants were waiting for Rebecca's arrival. The older of the two said, "Hold on a minute, and we will get you settled." They did so in very quick time and took Rebecca down the corridor. Margie went back to the car and drove it over to the parking area away from the main entrance. She carried Rebecca's packed bag into the reception area and asked where she should wait. She was directed down another corridor to the maternity area where quite a few males were pacing nervously. She felt a bit out of place, but after all, she was Rebecca's best friend and would stay there until the baby arrived.

One by one the pacing, coffee-drinking males were taken through the big heavy-duty plastic swing doors to the inner sanctum. When the doors swung open there were sounds from beyond from women in labour that made some of the men look like they were going to be sick or faint or both. On one level it amused Margie that men were supposed to be the stronger sex, but from where she was sitting in the maternity waiting area, it didn't appear to be correct.

Though she was happy for Rebecca, she couldn't help but feel sad for herself that she had not yet managed to get to a delivery room but consoled herself with the thought that she and Ron were still young and had plenty of time. At long last, after what seemed to be a lifetime, her name was called out, and she was ushered to a side room where Rebecca had been installed in a bed and beside her was a pink wrapped bundle. Margie rushed over and threw her arms around her shoulders. "Is it a girl?" she asked.

"Yes, all seven pounds twelve ounces of her, and her name is Amanda Marguerite, Amanda, after my favourite grandma, and Marguerite after you."

"Oh, Rebecca, how did you know my real name is Marguerite?"

"Because I asked Ron, you silly girl. You didn't think you weren't going to get a mention after all you have done for me, did you?"

The two friends hugged each other tight, both with tears in their eyes, and then pulled back the blanket to look at the latest addition to their world. Amanda Marguerite yawned, pushed one fist up out of the blanket, and opened her dark eyes to inspect these people who were disturbing her rest. Her little face seemed to say, "For goodness sake, can't a girl get her beauty sleep?" and the two young women laughed. Two days later Ron and Margie went to the hospital to take Rebecca and Amanda home.

While Rebecca and Amanda still shared her home, Margie had two more traumatic miscarriages but finally went almost full term with a little boy, but he was very sick with heart problems and not expected to live. She and Ron were absolutely devastated when their baby son died of complications within twenty-four hours. Her grief was incalculable, and Ron couldn't find the words to help her, as he was grieving too.

Over the next few years Margie and Ron reluctantly agreed that they couldn't face another pregnancy and the possibility of a miscarriage or a child who died before they could take him/her home. It was just more than either of them could cope with and it was causing cracks in their marriage as they retreated emotionally from each other.

They looked on Amanda as the child they would never have but were mindful that she was Rebecca's child, not theirs. They were both good, kind people, and so they vowed to do whatever they could to help Rebecca raise Amanda who was now four years old. She had grown into a truly delightful child; full of fun and mischief, always asking questions and wanting to learn. She had black curly hair like her mother and big brown eyes that shone with intelligence. She delighted in sitting with Ron each night while they drew pictures and made up stories about her day. Rebecca was always there at night to read Amanda a bedtime story and then tuck her in for the night. After that ritual, Margie and Ron would go in and say their goodnights to this little girl they loved so much.

Rebecca had an early-morning job in a bakery but finished about three. She was able to collect Amanda from pre-school and then, later on, from school. Ron, Margie, Rebecca, and Amanda always had dinner together and after Amanda was in bed Rebecca left for her second job cleaning nearby offices. It was a gruelling schedule, but Rebecca wanted to make a success of her life, and as much as she was grateful to Margie for the roof over their head, she wanted a place of her own.

Chapter 14

Margie knew that Rebecca was ambitious and would eventually move out to her own place, but she also knew that she would miss her company and would especially miss Amanda. There was tension sometimes between the two women over issues of discipline. To Margie's way of thinking Rebecca seemed to be too hard on Amanda, but she could also see that the little girl was sometimes confused about whom to go to and what to ask. Overall, however, they all got along well and Margie and Ron delighted in taking Amanda down the park for an hour or so to give Rebecca time to have her hair done or to catch up on some much-needed sleep. It was their time with this little girl that they could push on the swings, slide down a slippery dip with her or climb on the frames in the park.

It was a long time since Rebecca had mentioned her mother, and when Margie first broached the subject she was rather saddened by Rebecca's reply. "She knows where I am if she wants to see me." Margie tried to get the point over that there was a grandma out there somewhere who hadn't even seen her granddaughter. Rebecca just gave her a look that silenced Margie and the subject was never mentioned again.

When Amanda reached her tenth birthday, Rebecca had saved enough for a deposit on a home of her own. Margie was happy that she had achieved her goal but was also sad that they would be leaving what had been their home for nearly eleven years. Margie couldn't face seeing Rebecca's car pull away from the kerb following the removalist van to her new address. It was bad enough that Rebecca was moving, but it was heartbreaking for Margie that Amanda was going too. Ron stood on the front path and waved as Amanda sadly looked through the back window. She would miss Ron and Margie, but she was a child and had to go wherever her mother took her. Two minutes and they were no longer visible.

They went inside with their arms around each other with tears running down their cheeks. A little more than a decade had come to an end, and now there was just the two of them in what felt like a very empty house. They would just have to make the best of it, but fate had different ideas.

Over the last fifteen years Ron and Margie had slowly grown apart. Margie was no longer interested in the intimate side of their relationship, and that caused friction between them. The gulf widened even more after Rebecca and Amanda moved out. Their marriage had been reduced to polite conversation and separate bedrooms. This was not what they had planned all those years ago when as a young married couple they had moved into the house full of joy. Time and trauma had taken that away from them.

They no longer had their two favourite people living with them and bringing joy to the household. They missed not having Amanda bounce in every afternoon, throwing her school bag just inside the door before asking, "What's to eat?" Margie missed Rebecca's company more than she thought possible and wondered if she had pushed Ron away by spending more time with her friend than her husband.

Margie and Rebecca had kept in touch by phone and letter. Rebecca was as supportive as she could be from a distance, but she didn't have the money to travel from interstate to see Margie. She was also mindful that Ron had been a friend too and didn't want to take sides. Amanda was doing well at school and they often received a copy of an award or school certificate through the mail. Margie took the opportunity during a phone call to ask if she could speak to Amanda, but she always seemed to be at an after school activity or at a friend's house doing homework. Margie was sad that the threads of her friendship with Rebecca seemed to be shredding due to the tyranny of distance and living very different lives than they did when they shared a house, but she badly missed her friend and daughter. They had been the cornerstones of her life for so long.

Margie was lonely but couldn't find a way out of her depression. She could hardly be bothered to have a conversation with Ron that didn't include "What do you want for dinner?" or, "What time will you be home?" It was a sad time for them both. They had both run out of interest in each other; their passion was spent, and their lives had taken different paths. They no longer went on holidays together as they couldn't even agree on where they should go. Their weekends were spent pursuing different interests and their paths only crossed when they were home for meals and neither of them was happy.

Ron came to Margie one day and said, "I want a divorce, Margie. I can't live like this anymore, and I want to move on with my life. I am not happy, and neither are you." She wasn't really surprised, but it was the final nail in the coffin of their marriage.

"Go ahead and organise it," Margie replied, "I won't fight you. I am too tired and dispirited, and I know we have no future together."

Her marriage was over, her house was to be sold, and she now had to find a new path to tread for the rest of her life. She wasn't sure how she would do that, but she knew she would survive and move on. She had friends who had been divorced and they had managed to make a new life for themselves. She didn't see any reason why that would not be so for her. She would miss being half of a couple, but when she actually thought about it, she hadn't been in that situation for quite a few years. They just happened to be two people who had been married for a long time.

It was heartbreaking for both of them to sell the house that they had moved into as a young couple all those years ago. The house had been built for a family, but the distress and disappointment that accompanied each miscarriage, and the death of the only live baby Margie managed to deliver, was just too much, and their marriage had collapsed under the strain.

Margie had not been in the nursery since it had been dismantled and everything given away to charity so as not to remind her of what hopes had been dashed to the ground. The room had never been made into anything at all as Margie couldn't be bothered to give it another purpose. The real estate agent decided to call it a study, and as far as Margie was concerned they could call it anything they liked as long as she and Ron managed to sell their house of broken dreams.

They were given a list of things that needed to be improved before the house was put on the market and it was not of interest to either of them. Margie called up a home handyman service and had the painting and repairs done, paid the bill, and let the real estate know it was ready to sell. Price and a marketing campaign were agreed upon, she and Ron signed the papers and packed up their individual possessions ready for storage.

They agreed that they would split the profits 50/50. This seemed reasonable to Margie, and she duly signed on the bottom line of any papers that Ron put in front of her. She couldn't even be bothered to read them, let alone check out the fine print. She knew that Ron would be fair, as he had been all their married life.

The day of the auction brought many people, and the house was sold for $20,000 more than Margie and Ron had stipulated as the lowest price they would accept. This would give them both a chance to start again in their new life. There was no animosity between them, just regret that things hadn't worked out, but they didn't want to spend the rest of their lives going through the motions of a life together.

In the weeks following the auction, the surplus furniture was sent to a charity store, personal belongings distributed to their new abodes, and the key handed over to the real estate agent. It was a surreal moment when they shut the door of the house they had shared for more than twenty years and walked down the path together but left in separate cars, each to their new life.

Chapter 15

Ron had decided to rent an apartment for a while until he determined what he wanted to do with his life. He felt that he needed a complete change in his career, his lifestyle, and his future plans. There would not be enough money from the sale of the house to buy another one, and his heart wasn't in it anyway. He just needed somewhere to stay for however long it took to get back on his feet.

Margie had always had a yearning to own a shop so for the last twelve months she had been attending a local evening college to learn Small Business Management. She had never managed a business, and she knew that most people didn't plan to fail, they just failed to plan, and she wasn't about to lose her money through lack of knowledge. She knew this was her chance to have a new life and be part of the community.

Margie had found a small coffee shop in the next town that was for sale. It was a bit rundown because the previous owner had been sick, but she felt she could make a go of it. The clincher was that the shop came with a small residence on top that consisted of a bedroom, bathroom, sitting area, and a kitchen/laundry. She hadn't wanted to take any of the furniture from the house, as she wanted a fresh start.

Ron felt the same way and as he was going to rent, the furniture available would be too big for the apartment.

The same handyman who had helped Margie with the house refurbishment was employed to sort out the flat above the shop. The owner had let it become shabby as was the shop but Margie couldn't move into something that looked so worn and tired. The carpets were replaced, walls and doors repainted, furniture purchased, and it was ready for its new owner.

On the way to her newly renovated home, Margie had bought a few bunches of flowers to put in vases to cheer the place up a little, and a bottle of wine for her to celebrate with that night. She didn't particularly like drinking alone but, in this case, there was no one to share it with and she hoped that would change in the future.

She felt worn out and worn down with the effort of selling the house and after her divorce she was an emotional wreck. She hoped that the coffee shop would allow her to meet some new friends and get involved in the community she had moved into.

Margie had the sort of face that people instantly responded to. She had the usual number of wrinkles and grey hairs that someone in her age group was entitled to, but her eyes had the sparkle of someone much younger. She had closed the coffee shop down for a week as it needed a really good clean and she had put a sign in the window saying, "Grand Opening – New Owner" and the date. Many times when she was cleaning she noticed a few people peering in the window and when Margie waved, they waved back with a smile on their face. She felt welcome in this new community when she went to the local shops and she was greeted with "Are you the new owner of the coffee shop?" Everyone was interested in what she was planning for the future and it boded well for a successful reopening.

The coffee shop had been painted a dreary brown inside but had beautiful terracotta tiles on the floor; however, they were a devil to keep clean, as Margie soon found out. It was about this time that she decided she would use some of her savings to completely strip the floor back and seal it so it was easier to look after, plus paint the walls a soft yellow. She had decided on a Mexican theme because she could use lots of colours in the chairs, table covers, and the rustic-style china she had decided to buy inexpensively from a clearance company that specialised in this type of decorating.

She had noticed that there was an art school nearby, and she thought they might want to display some of their paintings for sale in the coffee shop. That would serve two purposes—decorate the walls and may make some money for the students.

The day of the grand opening arrived, and Margie was all ready. The tables and chairs were freshly painted, the walls were showing off the many art works that had been chosen, and their prices were neatly printed on cards next to them. New menus had been made up and placed in the middle of each table.

Two girls had been employed on a part-time basis, as they already had experience working in a coffee shop. She had asked them to come in the day before so she could make sure they knew what was expected of them. Neat and tidy was top of the list, no chewing gum, and if they had to wear coloured nail polish it was not to be chipped. The two girls thought Margie was a bit of a nitpicker, but they went along with it because they needed the job and she seemed a nice person.

The doors were opened at eight as Margie had noticed quite a few people walking by on their way to work at about that time. It was a good move because she had a very busy first hour with takeaway coffees and most times the customer also bought something to eat from the limited range available in the first week. Margie was planning to build up the range of food available for takeaway but just wanted to see what people preferred before she invested too much money and perhaps wasted more than she could afford. She was very glad that she had done her small business management course as it had given her confidence in her first venture.

The first day's takings were more than Margie had hoped for, and the comments from the customers about the new décor were very positive. They seemed to like the freshness of the shop and the paintings on the walls were a talking point. Many of them took a frequent sipper card so they could get their tenth coffee free after purchasing nine.

The vibes were good, and her two part-time workers really stepped up to the mark. They looked good, passed Margie's neat and tidy checklist each day, and were pleasant to the customers no matter how busy they became. They were also learning a lot about food preparation and handling, and so their skills increased.

Margie was exhausted by the end of the week but elated at the success, which was evidenced in the takings from the till. She was hopefully on her way to becoming a successful businesswoman. Ron phoned her on the Saturday to see how she was doing and what she thought of being a business owner. She was really excited about her week and was talking and talking and then said,

"Are you okay? You sound rather quiet." He just laughed and told her it would have been hard to get in a word anyway, but he was pleased with her success.

"I am just a bit lonely, but I will settle in to my new place soon," he assured her. "There are lots of people in the apartment block and the communal area and pool get used a lot on weekends so I have met some of the residents." Margie was happy for him, but she felt that she was talking to a stranger, not the man she had spent half her life with. It was a very weird feeling.

She had also employed a helper in the kitchen for the busiest time of the day and this had proved to be successful as well. The wages were more than fair; the staff all got along with each other and liked Margie. She worked harder than any of them and they could sense that their employment was likely to be long term if the shop proved to be the winner everyone predicted.

Previously the shop had closed at four each day, but Margie decided to try keeping it open for another hour. She let the girls go at three, and they looked as though they were glad to get off their feet. The previous owner had been unwell and that was probably the reason for the short hours, but Margie was hale and hearty, lived upstairs, and wasn't afraid of hard work. To her it was exhilarating, and she met each day with a spring in her step.

She had a few people come in who commented that they were glad the shop was open that extra time for a late-afternoon coffee and snack. Margie felt she was onto a winner. She had also noticed that mothers and children tended to come in after school and so she set up a corner where the children could play with some toys and let their mothers have a coffee with friends. It was a appealing idea and many of the mums congratulated her and said, "You must really know what makes children tick" and Margie forced herself to put on a smile and just nodded, but her heart still ached. She wished that Rebecca was still close by to share her joy.

She still missed Rebecca and Amanda and had no idea where they were now. The house they had first moved into had been sold because Rebecca found that it needed a lot of work and money spent on it that she just didn't have to spare. They had moved around a lot, renting places in different towns all over the State, and Margie's last letter had come back with "Return to Sender" written on the front and no other explanation. It was her dearest wish that their paths would cross again one day.

Ron had decided to take his share of the money and move to the city. He and Margie spoke on the phone every few weeks for a while, but sadly they no longer had anything in common to talk about. She most missed having a man around when she finally went upstairs at the end of the day and had her meal by herself. She didn't even have an animal to greet her but would put that right when she had some time to go to the local shelter. Some sort of cat would do nicely.

Chapter 16

The shop didn't trade on Sunday. Margie had tried it for the first two months, but it wasn't worth opening for the handful of people who came in. Once Margie had time to get herself a cat she went off to the shelter. She wasn't looking for anything specific but thought she would know the right one when she saw it. Margie was unaware that you don't choose a cat; a cat chooses you.

She spent some time looking in the cages but just couldn't find the right one, the one that looked as though it might be friendly, have a coat that was easy to care for and a bit of personality. Margie was almost ready to give up and was in the open area where older cats were housed when a male roused himself from his carpeted perch and batted at Margie's hair, which was level with his elevated position. Well that certainly got her attention.

She swung around to be confronted by a black cat with the biggest yellow eyes she had ever seen. He had a white front, much like a dinner suit, and a very imperious look about him. Once he had Margie's attention, he crept forward on his perch and stretched his head out so she could pat him. Margie fell in love with Prince. One of the workers at the shelter made the comment, "He will be the boss, you know" and Margie didn't mind a bit.

Prince was paid for, housed in a cage that he immediately resented, for the trip home and made his feelings known by yowling all the way. When they got home he investigated his new abode, took up residence on a chair that had the afternoon sun pouring down on it, and went to sleep. There was no need for him to establish his territory, and he just strolled around the flat, sniffing and looking to see what else there was in his new residence.

That night Margie decided to try brushing him to keep his fur nice and put him on her lap where he settled down while she groomed him, and he then fell asleep. Prince had found his forever home, and Margie was more than happy to have him there. She had company at last.

The coffee shop was proving to be a growing success. Margie was working long hours and for the first time in many years she was happy. She had a purpose to her days, which had been missing for some time, and she looked forward to opening the doors each morning at eight. She was building up quite a good clientele in the morning for coffee and snacks as takeaway. Midmorning, some young mothers with their children would settle down for a chat for an hour or so on their way to or from their exercise class. Margie was glad to have them there, but it brought back sad memories that she just had to put at the back of her mind.

Lunch was always busy, and Margie decided to put in a selection of sandwiches that were packed to go, and these too were a real hit. Some customers even rang in their order so they could just collect their food and take it back to work. She was thrilled with the way the business was building up and she was looking for ways to improve the food they could provide when Caroline came into the shop.

Chapter 17

As the weeks slipped into months, Caroline and Owen had seemed to find a balance in their life together. They refined their morning routine so they weren't late for work, stayed home on the weekend while Owen read the papers and Caroline did all the housework and washing, and didn't go out unless there was a free event somewhere.

They had never talked about birth control or children, just another subject that had been avoided, so when Caroline suspected she might be pregnant she wasn't quite sure how to deliver this information. She didn't know how Owen would take the news and had learned to fear his reactions to unpleasant subjects or events. The first thing to do was get a pregnancy test kit from the chemist. She couldn't believe her eyes when the results came back positive—she was going to have a baby.

Caroline made the evening cup of tea that they ritually had in the lounge room while they watched the news, and just blurted out, "I'm pregnant."

That will get his attention.

Owen's face swung away from the news on television and with a look of horror he said, "You're what? How did that happen? I didn't say I wanted a child and anyway we can't afford one."

Caroline just put her cup and saucer carefully down on his mother's side table, looked him straight in the eye and said, "Too late, there is one on the way."

For once he was without words.

They passed the rest of the evening in silence but a silence laden with anger, on Owen's part anyway. Caroline was secretly delighted but took care to not show her joy. She was slowly realising that perhaps Owen had mental health issues that she did not have the experience to recognise. She thought back to how loving her parents had been to each other, their affection and gentle touches as they passed each other and knew that this would not be the case with her marriage.

She knew, even at this early stage, that if she upset Owen she would pay a price in terms of his treatment of her. Ignoring her as if she were not even in the room was one of his specialities. She was not prepared to put her wellbeing in jeopardy with the new life growing within her. She knew she would have to tread carefully. The feelings in the household were at opposite ends of the spectrum. Owen was angry and Caroline was euphoric. She was delighted that she was having a child and vowed that it would be loved and wanted, as she had been, and she would give her child whatever she could, even with the financial constraints.

Owen didn't demand his husbandly rights when they went to bed and for that she was grateful. Whether he found her repulsive because she was carrying his child, or if he was so angry that he couldn't bear to be near her, she didn't care. For the first time since she had become Mrs Owen Brewster, she slept on her side of their bed without being bothered by her husband's sexual demands.

The next morning she was violently ill, as can be the case within the first three months of pregnancy, but Owen's comment was "Well, with a bit of luck you might lose it and we can go back to being a couple." She hadn't realised just how deep was his resentment about this growing human being, and it just made her more determined that she would do everything in her power to have this child and give it a good life, with or without the father that didn't want its existence to become real.

Her pregnancy proceeded, and Owen chose to ignore her slowly growing belly. He made no comment except to say, "Don't bother to buy too much for this thing, because we can't afford it." She was horrified that he called *her* baby a "thing," and she certainly thought of it as her baby and didn't really acknowledge Owen's part in the conception. He had made it abundantly clear that he was not interested in this whole project and would rather she didn't speak of it in his presence.

Caroline tried to broach the subject of needing to spend money on baby equipment, and Owen came up with a very interesting list. As far as he was concerned "it" could be bathed in the rough cement laundry tub, could start its life in the deep bottom drawer of a chest in the second bedroom, and its other requirements could be sourced from the local charity shop. In Owen's warped mind, this would be a win/win situation. Caroline could get what was needed cheaply and the charity would also benefit, as would he when very little money was coming from his pocket.

He was not aware that most women, with their first child, were able to spend hours daydreaming about what this child would be—boy or girl? How to decorate the nursery? Generally neutral colours were decided on, which would be freshly painted, and the walls decorated with frescoes or individual cartoon animals. What colour clothes to choose? Maybe lemon, white, pale green would be nice and could be worn by either sex. None of this information was imparted to Owen. He had made it quite clear he was simply not interested and didn't see himself becoming a parent.

As Caroline proceeded further into her pregnancy, and her pants and tops became tighter, she broached the subject that she needed to buy some maternity clothes. This request was met with a frosty silence and the instruction that she should just let the seams out. With a bewildered shake of her head, Caroline just retreated to the bedroom. *It's obvious that he doesn't realise how uncomfortable tight clothing can be.*

Owen's behaviour about becoming a parent, whether he recognised the fact or not, was becoming more bizarre, but Caroline had no girlfriends she could discuss her concerns with. She was five months pregnant and was starting to show. She asked to speak with her boss and when she announced she was having a baby, she first looked amazed and then sympathetic.

"How are you feeling?" she asked Caroline.

"Okay, I guess, but I need to let you know that I will be leaving in eight weeks. I will be seven months by then"

"Why so early?" asked her boss "Are you having any problems?"

Caroline confirmed that she wasn't, but she wanted some time before she actually had her child. It did not escape her boss's notice that she had said "my," not "our," child.

She did not tell her boss that she had simply run out of clothes that fit her and would be going shopping to the local charity store to try to find something loose and comfortable that didn't cost very much, but it was certainly not something she would be able to wear to work.

Over dinner that night, she broke the silence and told Owen she had given in her notice and would be leaving work in eight weeks. He almost choked on his mouthful of food and exploded with "Why can't you work right up until it is born?" Caroline explained that she couldn't fit into any of her clothes and wouldn't be able to wear the cheap clothes available from the charity shop to work. Owen was not happy. He could see no reason why his wife should sacrifice two months pay just because she was having a baby. He hadn't been consulted about this pregnancy, her burgeoning belly revolted him, and the loss of her wage would seriously affect their weekly income.

"Other women managed to work in the fields and give birth squatting where they are in other countries" he informed Caroline. She replied that she didn't work in a field, had given her notice, which had been accepted.

I wish he was joking, but I know he isn't. What sort of life with this man lies ahead for my child and me?

Caroline's pregnancy was trouble free and she glowed with good health, which was fortunate because they had no health insurance. She was booked into the public system with a midwife, as there was no chance of her having an obstetrician of her choice. This was not in the spreadsheet of expenses drawn up by Owen.

After her announcement at the dinner table that she was leaving work in eight weeks, fifty dollars was reluctantly handed to Caroline the next morning with the instruction from Owen to spend it wisely as there would be no more for pregnancy clothing. "It" had not been his idea, and he wasn't wasting money on clothes that she would only wear for a few months. She put the money in her purse and later that morning went shopping but was not intending to spend it all on maternity clothes. Caroline had a plan.

She went down to the charity shop and bought a few tops and elasticised pants for twenty dollars for the lot, and hoped that would get her through to the end of her pregnancy. She didn't need to dress up for anyone, as they didn't go anywhere. Two tops and two pants were enough to get her through each week when she didn't have to show up for work every day and, when questioned by Owen, she explained that charity shops don't give receipts. He greeted this news with scepticism but was glad that she had managed to get some clothes for the very generous amount he had given her. The thirty dollars change was hidden in the back of Caroline's underwear drawer for future use.

Walking every day to the bus stop while she was still working had taken Caroline past a coffee shop that always had lots of customers. She had seen a sign in the window "home baking required." She had ventured in one day the week before and asked the friendly owner, Margie, what they needed. Margie had volunteered the information that their usual cookie supplier had folded up overnight because of family issues. They desperately needed someone immediately to bake cookies of four or five varieties for customers to have with their coffee. Caroline could do this! She had thirty dollars and could buy the ingredients for the first batch, and it wouldn't be noticed on the grocery bill. Margie and Caroline came to an agreement over the price, variety, and quantities. Caroline informed Margie that she was leaving work the coming Friday and would have cookies ready for her early next week. She hesitantly asked Margie "Just one thing. I was wondering if you could pay me for each batch on the day? I don't have any income and I don't want my husband to find out I am earning money he doesn't know about." Margie readily agreed and wondered who was the husband of this lovely young woman. She was obviously pregnant, not well dressed but very clean and tidy. Margie liked her on sight and hoped their arrangement worked out for both of them.

Don't worry baby, we will be fine. I will always look after you.

Little did Owen know that Caroline had kept the change of thirty dollars for flour, butter, sugar, and other biscuit ingredients. She had taken it from its original hiding place and was now hidden in the red kettle that he hated and would never touch, much less use to heat water. It was too much a reminder of the life Caroline had before she married him. She knew it was safe there, secreted away in plain sight. This was the start of her bid for freedom.

As far as Caroline was concerned, the best part of her pregnancy was that Owen didn't come anywhere near her. She had lost any affectionate feelings for him and was glad that he sat in the lounge watching television until Caroline had retired to bed. He informed her he was revolted to feel her belly pushing up against his back in the middle of the night, even though she was unaware of this happening. He couldn't stand to look at his formerly svelte wife with a watermelon-sized bump sticking out the front of her body. He found the whole process of pregnancy repulsive.

Friday came around and Caroline left work that day. There was a small collection from sympathetic workmates and a basket of generic baby goods for her. Nobody could understand how Owen had even managed to convince her to marry him, let alone conceive a child. He was seen as an insignificant person in a brown suit, in an office somewhere, doing a job nobody else wanted, who had married one of the best-looking girls in the office. Caroline would have been amazed to know that anybody thought she was good looking and that she could have had her choice of the single male population in her company. Her shyness and lack of dates had rendered her the perfect target for Owen, not to mention that she was an only child and her parents deceased, leaving her with money in the bank—a very attractive attribute.

Caroline kept her appointments with the public hospital midwives, and her pregnancy continued according to the textbook. She spent the last weeks taking good care of herself and putting in place her secret plan of earning some money to put away for the future of her baby.

I just don't see this man in my future, especially with his attitude towards my baby.

Caroline was elated when she returned home and, on the Monday morning after Owen had left for work, she sourced out some recipes that her mother had put aside in one of the memorabilia boxes. They were family-tested recipes that required few ingredients but were really tasty. Over the months she had been married, and particularly since she had been pregnant, Caroline had tried to introduce new food into their diet, but Owen had vehemently refused. All he wanted was the sort of food his mother had cooked so Caroline had put her mother's recipes away.

She worked out how many ingredients she could buy with the thirty dollars hidden in the red kettle, and calculated that she could make enough to meet Margie's requirements for a first order. As soon as she had her list worked out, Caroline went shopping. She managed to buy enough ingredients for an order of five different varieties of about two-dozen cookies of each type. She rang Margie and said that she would have the order to her late afternoon for the next day's trading. They had agreed that this first order would be a trial to see how the customers liked the variety and, if successful, Margie and Caroline would work out what was required over a week's trading.

She was so excited but was careful that she didn't show this emotion to Owen on his return from work. He would immediately suspect that she was up to something he would not approve of, and Caroline wasn't about to let him in on her secret so he could smash her dreams down once more. He would not be pleased that she had an enterprise of her own, particularly when it was funded by *his* thirty dollars.

Mid-morning Caroline spent two hours mixing and baking and delivered the cookies to Margie with enough time to clean up the kitchen and cook dinner for Owen's return at six. He expected his dinner on the table within ten minutes of his arrival home, which gave him enough time to wash his face and hands and watch the news headlines. He caught the same time train every day, his dinner was put on the table at the expected moment, and he ate it without comment. Caroline had learned not to expect any "Thanks, that was lovely" at the end of the meal. She just played the dutiful wife and cleared the table off, washed the dishes, and set the table for the next morning. By that time Owen had retired to the lounge room to watch the next lot of news broadcasts as he did every evening like clockwork.

Margie rang Caroline the next day to tell her that the cookies had been a great hit and that the supply was almost exhausted. She asked if Caroline could do a repeat order for the next day. Caroline was thrilled and secretly thanked her dear mother for these great recipes. She was starting to see that this could be the door opening to a new and different future for her.

Her marriage to Owen was not destined for longevity and she was concerned about his mental state. He only spoke to her when he had to and showed her no affection whatsoever. She was anxious about continuing to share a house with him, especially the way he felt about the impending arrival of a child whose existence he had not given permission for.

After Owen left for work the next morning, Caroline went into the laundry. When cooking the first order of cookies, she had mixed up a double lot of dough in the hope she would get another order from Margie. She had stored the plastic-wrapped cookies in the washing machine, as she knew she was in no danger of Owen looking in there for any reason. As far as he was concerned, his wife was now in charge of laundry. If this venture was to proceed, Caroline needed to buy some jars in order to keep the baked cookies fresh for delivery. That would be her next purchase but before anything else she had to get this next order to Margie.

The cookies were packed into a cardboard box that Caroline had saved from her belongings in the storage unit and she set off on her daily walk, carefully balancing the box on her growing belly. When she got to the coffee shop, Margie greeted her with enthusiasm. "You have my cookies?" Caroline confirmed that she did indeed have her cookies and was glad they had been well received.

Margie opened the box and said, "Oh my, they look delicious. These are going to be a great hit with the customers." Caroline was happy that her first order had been a success and the money was all hers. More dollars were hidden in the red kettle.

Margie and Caroline organised how many cookies should be baked and when they could be delivered. Caroline asked, "I would rather nobody know where these cookies are coming from. I will be in trouble if my husband finds out". Margie was a woman of the world and understood that husbands didn't need to know everything, so readily agreed that it would be "just between us girls." And so the cash from the second delivery went into the red kettle. Everything from now on was profit.

Caroline realised that she could only put notes in the red kettle because coin could make a noise if Owen happened to move it, even though he hated the sight of it. As soon as she got coin she changed it into notes. When the smaller notes made up one hundred dollars, she changed it into a larger note. Her little nest egg was growing, as was the beloved child in her belly.

For the last weeks of her pregnancy Caroline baked cookies almost every day. They were so popular at Margie's Coffee Shop that it was difficult to keep up with demand, but by mixing up the biscuit dough the afternoon before and stashing it in the ugly twin-tub washing machine, she managed to start baking as soon as Owen left for the office each morning. The hundred-dollar notes in the red kettle were steadily increasing, but Caroline knew she had to find somewhere else to stash her money, as it was too unsafe having it in the house. She couldn't risk opening a bank account in her name, because if Owen collected the mail before she had a chance to, he would have no hesitation in opening anything addressed to her – especially if it had a bank logo on the envelope. If Owen found out she didn't want to think what the consequences would be for her, especially with his temper outbursts being interspersed with ignoring her totally.

I will have to find somewhere else to hide my nest egg.

Margie had become a friend to Caroline, and she appreciated the older woman's insight on what made the world go around. At the end of one cookie delivery Margie asked Caroline, "What are you saving up for?"

"Freedom."

Margie was a bit taken aback by her reply but chose not to ask as she suspected that Caroline was not happy in her marriage but didn't want to interfere. She just wanted to be her friend and gave her a card with her mobile number written on it. "If you ever need help, please phone me. I will always stand by you". Caroline was really touched and gratefully took the card and put it in her purse with the response "Thanks, Margie. I really appreciate that."

When Caroline got home she put Margie's card behind Hurry's ashes at the back of her underwear drawer. She hoped she wouldn't need it, but she knew where she could contact a friend if ever she did. It made her feel a little more secure in her insecure world with Owen, who seemed to be becoming more mentally unhinged.

Chapter 18

Owen had refused to go to any prenatal classes or discuss what Caroline had learned. Caroline was still trying to get him to at least acknowledge that they were going to be three in the not-too-distant future. After all, she reasoned, he was responsible for the sperm that had combined with her egg to produce this baby. Her husband refused to discuss names for the child, whichever sex it was, and was ignoring its imminent arrival.

Earlier in her pregnancy, Caroline asked Owen for ten dollars extra housekeeping money so she could buy some wool from the charity shop and after complaining long and loud he handed over the requested amount. She happily sat each evening in the lounge room knitting booties and tiny jackets. Owen deliberately angled himself away from this exhibition of nesting instinct and seemed to concentrate very hard on what was on the television. Caroline was not sure whether to laugh or cry at his ridiculous antics.

He showed no interest in what she was knitting so she just finished each piece and lovingly wrapped it in tissue paper and stored it away, ready for her child's arrival. Owen suggested that she might like to sleep in the second room as her tossing and turning each night was keeping him awake and he needed to be sharp each day for his job.

Caroline was not disappointed about this arrangement because she preferred to sleep on her own as her belly got bigger and needed pillows underneath it so she could be comfortable.

On the Saturday morning five days before her due date, she felt very uncomfortable. Her back was aching and she thought it was time she went to the hospital. She told Owen that she thought "it was time" and he momentarily moved his eyes from the newspaper and said, "So? What do you expect me to do?"

Caroline suggested that he call a taxi so she could go to hospital. "I am not wasting money on a taxi. It was your idea to get pregnant, not mine. If you are in labour then you need to get yourself to hospital." And he went back to reading the paper.

She didn't dare go to the red kettle and take some money out, so she rang Margie. Caroline knew it was a busy morning and hated to ask a favour, but she could hardly go on the bus with the risk of her waters breaking during the journey. Margie arrived within minutes and knocked on Caroline's door. Owen answered the door and asked, "Who are you?"

"A friend of your wife." Margie pushed him aside and went to Caroline. She had disliked Owen on sight and wasn't prepared to have any conversation with him just now, especially with his attitude to the imminent arrival of his first child.

She settled Caroline in her car and drove very carefully to the hospital. Margie helped Caroline into the Maternity Admissions Department, gave the clerk her phone number, and asked them to call her when Caroline was about to give birth. They asked Margie who she was and she said, "I am her stepmother. Her mother is deceased." They recorded these details on Caroline's chart. All the boxes had to be ticked on the admission form so the question came up "And the father?" Margie quickly answered that he was overseas on business at the moment. The clerk's raised eyebrows indicated amazement that a father would be absent half a world away at the time his first child was due, but she reasoned it was none of her business.

Later that afternoon, Margie left her part-time girls in charge of the coffee shop and headed for the hospital. Caroline's labour was progressing well, according to the midwife, and Margie was allowed in to be with her for a short time. This brought back memories of looking after Rebecca when Amanda was born all those years ago.

It also brought tears to her eyes when she thought about her delivery of the only live child she had been able to bring into the world, but she swept them aside and concentrated on how her young friend was managing.

She held Caroline's hand when the pains got stronger and gently wiped her forehead with a cool cloth. The midwives advised that everything was going according to plan and Baby Brewster would be arriving within the next hour or so. After a few more strong contractions and some guttural noises from Caroline, Baby Brewster made his way safely into the world with quite a lusty yell. "What have I got?" Caroline asked.

"A good strong healthy baby boy," answered the midwife as the new mother collapsed back on the pillows with a big smile on her face. Margie had never seen someone else give birth before, and she was overcome with emotion. She alternated between laughing and crying, with a lot of hugging of Caroline. They were both delighted with the dear little boy that had been born, and Caroline announced his name would be Gavin, "Did Owen choose that name?" asked Margie.

"No, I did. It was my father's middle name". Caroline just said that Owen wasn't interested in this child at all. She didn't see the sad look that passed across Margie's face, and, in that moment, Margie promised herself that she would do all she could for this lovely young woman, who was now a new mum.

Margie arranged to collect her friend from the hospital the next morning, and she would drive her home. Caroline was very grateful for this as the thought of getting on a bus with a new baby was a bit daunting to say the least. At the appointed time Margie arrived at the front of the hospital and gently helped Caroline into the front seat. A borrowed baby capsule was firmly anchored in the back seat, and Caroline wondered where on earth Margie had managed to get that at such short notice.

When they pulled up outside Caroline's address Margie helped her out and then handed Gavin to her. She extracted a large cardboard box from the boot and walked up the path with mother and son and knocked on the front door, which was opened by Owen. "I have brought your wife and son home," she announced in her forthright manner. With a firm elbow delivered by Margie into his solar plexus, Owen was pushed aside while Margie ushered the new little family into the hall, but the look on his face was one of anger. Margie just ignored him and Caroline wasn't looking at him so it was a waste of time. Margie had dealt with his sort in business and wasn't impressed by his pettiness.

She dumped the cardboard box on the nearest flat surface, which happened to be the dining table, and informed Owen that it was full of baby stuff, second-hand admittedly but all washed and in good order. Caroline and her son were safely home, and Margie was going to keep a very good eye on both of them. She suspected stormy times ahead for Caroline, but she wouldn't be riding out those storms alone.

A day had gone by, and Owen still hadn't even looked at his son. Caroline was a bit disappointed but by now not really surprised at his attitude. She had come to the realisation that the only two things Owen loved were money and himself, probably in that order. She didn't figure in the equation and neither did her beloved baby. Owen had made it quite clear that he wanted nothing to do with this baby that he hadn't been consulted about, and he wouldn't be giving Caroline extra housekeeping either. She informed him that she would be getting money from the government in the form of a child allowance, and it was his moral duty to support her and her baby.

She was sick of being bullied by this short, boring, balding little man and any feelings she might have had for him had long since disappeared. She bluffed him by saying that she would write to the Human Resources Department of his company and let them know in no uncertain terms that he had refused to support his wife and child. He went pale and sweaty, because he wouldn't want anyone to know his private business and he wasn't entirely sure that Caroline wouldn't do what she threatened.

He correctly suspected that Margie had somehow managed to strengthen Caroline's backbone, and the meek woman he married had disappeared when she had become a mother. She had taken on the protective instincts of a lioness, and he wasn't at all sure he liked the new Caroline. He knew that by law it would cost money to get rid of her, and he didn't see that as a good investment, especially if he had to pay extra for that child of hers.

He agreed to increase the housekeeping by twenty per cent but told Caroline that whatever she didn't spend during the week she was to give back to him. In Caroline's mind there was never going to be any change, and if there was it would go in the red kettle.

Does he think I was born yesterday?

She reasoned that a child only needs one good parent and Gavin had that, so he would be okay, and with Margie as a surrogate grandmother she would build a new life for herself and her child. Women had been managing children by themselves for centuries when they were widowed young or their men went off to war, and there was no reason she couldn't do it too. She had had wonderful loving parents and was going to bring Gavin up the same way. She had so much more confidence since she had known Margie and knew that there was someone in the world who cared about her wellbeing.

Chapter 19

As Caroline had been relegated to the second bedroom when pregnant, she decided she would stay there. She had no desire whatsoever to move back into the marital bed, and she rather liked having Gavin close by in his bassinet, bought with a few dollars from the local charity shop. She had unpacked the box given to her by Margie and inside were some lovely little outfits in lemon, white, pale green, and blue. She was so thrilled that somebody had bothered to think of her and her son in such a loving way and quietly shed a few tears of joy. She dressed him in one of her own hand-knit garments, over a little sleep suit that Margie had given her, and was so proud of how beautiful he looked.

Gavin was a good baby and fed regularly, sleeping quietly in his bed with his tiny fists clenched and pushed up under his face. She couldn't stop looking at this little miracle and loved to touch his velvety skin and smell that unique baby smell—a mixture of soap from his bath and burped milk. She enjoyed putting the baby brush over his silky hair and adored everything about this little person who had come into her formerly bleak and lonely life.

The cookie orders had to continue if Caroline was ever going to have a life without Owen. She cooked his meals, washed his shirts, socks, and jocks and cleaned the house. Their conversations were stilted and consisted of "What would you like for dinner?" and "What time will you be home?" the latter probably irrelevant as he always came home on the same time train each evening, but it broke the silence.

The gas bill got his attention. It was almost double the one for the previous quarter. Caroline had anticipated this and so explained that she was using hot water for the nappies and baby clothes and that she was cooking more casseroles and desserts so used extra gas. He wasn't sure that she was telling the truth, but he couldn't prove otherwise so just took the bill and put it in the "To Pay" file hanging on the back of the kitchen door. He would be keeping an eye on this type of extravagance now that the child had arrived.

He was determined that he wouldn't have anything to do with him and refused to even look at his son. This saddened Caroline, but by now she didn't expect anything different from Owen. He seemed to be devoid of feelings unless it was about money, and he had certainly managed to get all that she had earned and inherited and deposited it where it was difficult, if not impossible, to access.

Selling Betty had been the final nail in the coffin of this marriage. He knew how much she loved that car and had let her keep Betty until the storage unit had been emptied, probably because he didn't want to pay for a removalist. It would have been so handy now to have the car to take her cookies to Margie, but Caroline would find a way to keep her orders going out and the money coming in. She had a plan, and it didn't include her husband. However, she knew she wouldn't be able to even broach the subject of a car.

I will manage, no matter how difficult he makes it. I have my freedom to work for.

Owen was totally unaware that with the money from the refund on the storage unit Caroline had bought a microwave oven, which she had hidden under her bed. It meant that Caroline could cook up a big casserole, freeze some of it, defrost and reheat it just before Owen was due home, and miraculously present it as a piping hot meal. This was especially helpful on an evening when she had been baking cookies, and it just meant putting the reheated casserole in the oven after taking the cookies out. The smell of the casserole soon rid the kitchen of the cookies smell. It had never been in her nature to be devious, but if that was what it took to extricate her from the present situation then so be it.

When the cookies were due each week, Caroline pushed the pram (a gift from one of Margie's customers) down to the shops and had utilised the big carry bag on the back to accommodate the cookies. She dropped them off, did her shopping, and was home in time to get another batch ready to be stored in the washing machine. Necessity is the mother of invention, as the saying goes.

Gavin was a good baby and slept while he was in his pram on daily walks. Caroline was keeping quite fit walking backwards and forwards to the coffee shop each day, then doing the shopping. She was still wearing her maternity clothes, as she didn't want to raise any red flags about where she got money to buy post-pregnancy clothes. That would have to wait.

The cookies were such a hit in the coffee shop that Margie started to sell them in little gift bags as well and so a few more dollars came in. The disadvantage was that Caroline could only bake a certain amount in the time she had available, in between looking after Gavin and doing all the chores. The other issue was the gas bill— more cookies meant more gas used and Caroline would find it very difficult to explain the increase. She had gotten away with it the first bill received after her cookie cooking commenced, but she doubted that another increase would be readily accepted. Owen would not have his household turned upside down for any reason. He expected there to be no blips on the radar of a perfectly run home now that his wife wasn't working and he was the sole supporter. If only he knew!

Margie and Caroline put their heads together and came up with a plan. If Caroline could make up large batches of biscuit dough, then Margie would store them in the industrial-sized refrigerator at the coffee shop. They could be packaged and marketed as "Dough to Go - just 10 minutes in the oven," thus removing the problem of Caroline's gas bill climbing to unexplainable heights. Margie went about sourcing out the advertising material and the regulations for storing this type of food. Caroline and Margie spent a long time brainstorming names for their new venture and decided to combine their names … and so Caromar Cookies was born.

--oOo--

Chapter 20
Amanda

AMANDA Watkins started work with a multinational company just after she finished a business degree at university. She was only twenty-one years old but was intelligent, a hard worker, and wasn't prepared to be on the bottom rung of the ladder for very long. For four years Amanda took extra courses to improve her skills, attended seminars in different parts of the company, and even went to Paris on a trip.

She was a tall, dark-haired and good-looking young woman, thanks to her Spanish father, and she attracted a lot of attention from the males in the company. Amanda, however, had made it a personal rule to never date anyone she worked with and especially the boss. If things went pear shaped it would be Amanda who got fired, not the boss. This was not going to happen to her.

However, that was before Damien joined the company. He was ten years older than her, charming, very good looking, and ambitious. CEO of the company was where he aimed to be in ten years time, and he would do whatever it took to achieve his goal. He had been transferred from another branch of the company and apart from the official press release regarding his new appointment, nothing much was known about him on a personal level. He kept his private life very private.

He worked in a different department, and Amanda first became aware of his existence when the company had a conference for all the senior executives and invited people from their other branches overseas to come to Australia. Amanda was asked to help run the conference and was put in charge of hotel accommodation and transport for the executives. It was the biggest job she had ever been asked to do, but she was confident that she could get it right. The work pace was intense, but she willingly rose to the challenge.

Amanda worked longer hours for this conference than she thought humanly possible. Each night she went home to her pocket handkerchief-sized apartment and just fell into bed, without taking off her make-up, which was something Amanda didn't usually do. She was aware that this would not be good for her skin, but she was just too tired to bother. She would worry about the effect on her skin at some future point.

Each morning she was first in the office with a coffee in one hand and a snack in the other. She knew she wasn't being sensible with her food, but she just didn't have time to eat breakfast at home. By buying on the run she could save valuable minutes.

Amanda could have asked someone in the office to help her, but she didn't trust that they would do what was required correctly or on time. Most of the girls seemed to be forever on their mobile phones with friends or sending personal emails. This was something that Amanda didn't do but mainly because she had few friends. She was too busy trying to climb the corporate ladder to "do lunch" most days, as the other girls seemed to do. They were either getting ready to go out to lunch or coming back to the office a little the worse for wear after a few wines on board.

For two days Amanda went over lists of delegates, their arrival times, transport from the airport to the hotel, whether they had a room, a name tag for the conference and all the minutiae to be checked with regard to dietary requests, and seating arrangements such as "need to have an aisle seat." It was time consuming and physically taxing, but at the end of the conference everything that she had been in charge of had gone off without a hitch.

On the first morning of the conference Amanda was seated at the table set aside for handing out name tags and ticking off those delegates who had arrived. One such delegate was Mr Damien Connors. She found his nametag and the conference information pack and handed it to him. She looked up into his beautiful brown eyes, and when she handed him the conference pack, he smiled at her and said, "Where have you been hiding?"

He was gorgeous and Amanda was smitten. She just stammered in reply "I am in the Finance Department." He just nodded and gave her another thousand-watt smile.

When the conference was over Amanda went back to her usual work, but she was called into her boss's office and told that she had done an excellent job and they were very pleased with her. They had good feedback from several of the delegates that she was very helpful, efficient, and never lost her cool. She was also told that this would be taken into account at the next lot of salary reviews.

A few weeks after the conference Amanda was again called into her boss's office and asked if she would like to transfer to another department, which would be a promotion for her. They would be sorry to see her leave their department, but she had made it quite plain that if there were a promotion available she would like to be considered for the position. Scant details about the new position were available from her boss, but as far as Amanda was concerned a change was as good as a holiday and as long as it was one rung up the ladder she would give it her best shot.

She went to the Human Resources Department and discussed the position on offer. It was a much better salary and gave her more scope to improve her skills. She was contacted a week later and advised that she had been successful. Amanda asked, "Who will I be working for?" and was stunned when the answer was "Mr Damien Connors will be your boss. He is really nice and I am sure you will get along just fine." She was pleased that she had been successful but told herself again, "I don't date work colleagues – and especially the boss." But she had not reckoned on Damien's persistence.

It was some time later that Amanda found out that Damien had requested her transfer to his department. She was annoyed that she hadn't got the job solely on her own merits, but it was because he wanted her to work for him. He had engineered the whole thing and as it turned out it was more for his benefit than Amanda's.

On the first day as his personal assistant, Amanda was instructed in what he expected of her. He told her that he worked hard, and he expected her to do the same. There might be mornings that she had to come in early or evenings when she was expected to work late. She assured him that this would not be a problem as she loved her job and lived alone quite close to work. He said that he would organise a car to take her home if she had to work late and they then talked about the other details of the job. Amanda was sure that it was quite within her capabilities, and she had just put her foot on the next rung of the corporate ladder.

Mr Damien Connors intrigued Amanda. Even though he got through an enormous amount of work each day, he never seemed to tire. His desk was pristine, except for whatever he was working on, with no photos of females, children or pets, and his out-of-hours life remained a mystery. He didn't ask Amanda about her personal life, and she certainly wasn't brave enough to venture asking about his.

Weeks turned into months, and Amanda loved her job just as much as she thought she would. All the staff in the department worked really hard, and the atmosphere was friendly and productive. A few of the males had tried to get Amanda to go out on a date, but she'd told them, "I don't date anyone where I work." They accepted her explanation as she had made her reasons quite clear. As far as anyone could work out, Amanda didn't do anything else but work. She was in the office before anyone else and was the last to turn out the lights. Most of the guys thought she was wasted, and the girls thought she was mad. They didn't have Amanda's ambition, but they didn't have her background either.

She had never told anyone that she was born as the result of a holiday fling when her mother went to Spain. The equation was good-looking guy and girl with too much alcohol on board = surprise baby when you get back from holiday. Some people bring back photos or diseases, but Rebecca (Amanda's mother) brought her back, albeit the size of a jellybean. By the time she realised she was pregnant Spain was a distant memory; Luis was unaware of his impending fatherhood and he was travelling with another group of tourists. As holiday flings go he had never tried to contact Rebecca and Amanda had never even seen a photo of her father.

Her mother had told Amanda that she had never even considered an abortion as that was against everything she believed in. She couldn't stay at home as her mother was absolutely furious at her for being so stupid as to get pregnant while on holiday. After her mother lost her job, Rebecca went to stay with her friend Margie and husband Ron, who took her in and looked after her. Rebecca had worked two jobs to support them both and so her work ethic was passed onto Amanda.

She had a lonely childhood as her mother worked as many hours as she could and vowed that her daughter would have a good education. Margie and Ron were like extra parents, but Rebecca always had the last word about her daughter's discipline. Rebecca was constantly looking for a better job to earn more money and this meant moving from city to city or state to state. For a few years they had managed to stay in touch by phone or letter, but as time went on the constant changing of addresses and phone numbers contact had been lost. Neither Amanda nor her mother was aware that Margie and Ron had divorced and gone their separate ways.

Rebecca managed to save enough money to put her daughter through university and this allowed her to start her career with the multinational company. The company was sending executives and their personal assistants overseas for a week to their head office in the UK. The trip details were sent through the internal email. She was off to London!

Amanda was nervous about the trip as she really didn't like flying, but it was a necessary part of her job. When they arrived at the hotel, keys were issued, and she realised that she would be staying on the same floor as her boss, the other executives, and their PA's.

He had always treated Amanda courteously, and she realised she didn't really know much about him. Amanda had heard whispers around the office that he and his wife weren't all that happy. How people knew this when they didn't even work for him Amanda couldn't quite figure out.

The first day they spent at the head office Damien and Amanda shared a taxi, and the conversation was a bit stilted. He asked her what she did when she wasn't working, and she commented that she really didn't have a life outside work. She just wanted to succeed and the only way that was going to happen was to work hard and be promoted. She wanted a career and wouldn't let anything stand in her way.

Dinner was to be held at the hotel they were all staying in and Amanda found herself sitting next to Damien. Throughout dinner they chatted amicably enough, but Amanda noticed that he was drinking quite a lot more than anyone else. Dinner finished and most of the others drifted off to the lounge to have a nightcap. Damien could hardly get up off his chair, so Amanda discreetly helped him across the foyer to the lift.

They were staying on the same floor so Amanda guided him to his room, searched his pockets for the keys, and virtually pushed him in the door and into the closest chair. This was no mean feat for someone as slightly built as Amanda. She didn't want any gossip about her spreading through the company when she was doing something as innocent as helping her boss to his room. The next morning, Damien came into breakfast looking a bit the worse for wear but nothing was said. He was, after all, the boss of the department and he could do whatever he liked.

They all met downstairs to wait for their transport. Amanda was smartly dressed, as usual, impeccably groomed and speaking quietly to Damien. When she had first been promoted several of the executives doubted that she could work as hard as Damien, but it didn't take long before they changed their minds. She was dedicated to her job and didn't mind longer hours to get the work done. Most of them were quite in awe of her energy and wished they had as much. Although, to be truthful, if they did have her energy they wouldn't be using it up at work.

Damien was speaking quietly to Amanda because he wanted to know how he had got back to his room the night before. She reassured him that everything was above board as she had helped him, left him sitting in the chair closest to the door, and gone to her own room. He seemed relieved and thanked her for taking care of him. His parting comment was "I am not really happy at home, Amanda, and sometimes I just drink too much."

The week seemed to go very fast and then it was back to the office. It was a twenty-four-hour trip from London to Sydney and most of the people were very tired by the time they got on the plane for the homeward journey. Amanda was horrified when she awoke to find that she had been sleeping with her head on her boss's shoulder. Damien told her not to worry, she had looked very peaceful, and she had deserved a good rest. He reassured her that he couldn't have done without her organisational abilities and her attention to detail while they were at the head office.

Amanda had taken copious notes of the proceedings and was going to make sure they were all typed up when she got back to her office. There was such a lot that they could do to improve the department, and Amanda wasn't about to waste what they had learned. Let everyone else just go about his or her business and stay in the same old groove, but that wasn't what she was about.

Two days after they arrived back, she asked to have a meeting with Damien so she could put forward a proposal for improvements. He was amazed that this young woman had taken the trouble to collate so much information and now presented it to him in a folder with her recommendations.

He took the time to read through the folder and as it was almost the end of the day he suggested they go out for dinner, on the company, as he would like to discuss some of her recommendations. Amanda hesitated, but he assured her it was a "working dinner" and he would see that she got home safely afterwards. She was of two minds about this "working dinner" but would see how it worked out.

After spending time with Damien on the trip to the head office she realised that she was developing feelings for him that were definitely not in her plan. She had to keep reminding herself, "I don't date anyone at work – and especially the boss." She knew he was married, but he never mentioned his wife, and she didn't really know whether he had children or not. Amanda was faced with a decision: Go out with Damien for a "working dinner" and see where it went, or try to get transferred somewhere else. She knew that she couldn't keep working with him when she felt the way she did. She knew she was in dangerous waters as she was very attracted to him but didn't know what to do about it.

Amanda was not experienced in dating, although she had been out on a few occasions and sometimes she'd still be with that person three months or six months later, but eventually she got bored or the passion just petered out. Damien was a whole different kettle of fish.

The "working dinner" turned out to be just that, and Amanda didn't know whether she was pleased or disappointed. They discussed her ideas in detail and it was obvious that Damien was happy with what she had put together. He assured her he would call a meeting of the other executives so that Amanda could present her recommendations. When dinner was over, Damien arranged for his company car to drop Amanda home, and then he would continue on. It was then that she realised she didn't even know where her boss lived.

The presentation went well, and Damien sent her a letter of congratulations and suggested that they go out for a drink to celebrate. It just happened to be Amanda's twenty-sixth birthday, but she didn't think he was aware of that, as birthdays were not generally celebrated in their department. There were so many people that it would have been drinks at least once a week, and Damien didn't encourage too much drinking. Long lunches were banned as he expected his colleagues to do a good day's work for a good day's pay. Anyone who didn't want to abide by his rules soon found himself or herself standing near the door marked Exit with a final payslip in their hand.

After weighing up the pros and cons, Amanda decided to go for just one drink to celebrate her birthday. She had received a card and gift from her mother, but it would be nice to have someone to share her special day with. Damien seemed pleased that she had decided in his favour rather than heading straight home to her lonely apartment. They went to a wine bar close to the office, tucked away in a side street and not likely to be visited by any of the staff. He had obviously been there before as he was greeted by name, and Amanda was rather surprised. He asked if she liked champagne, and when she said yes he motioned to the waiter who appeared in what seemed an instant, carrying an ice bucket with a bottle already opened and ready to be poured. The waiter filled their two glasses, and Damien held his up. "Happy Birthday, Amanda." Her eyes filled up with tears.

"Have I said something wrong?" asked Damien with concern in his voice.

"No, you just said something right and thank you for making my day special. I had no idea that anyone in the company knew my birth date."

They clinked glasses. "Thank you for all your hard work and dedication. I really appreciate it."

They chatted on about work and future plans for the department, staying away from personal subjects, as was Damien's way. As they were leaving the wine bar, he called a taxi for Amanda, and as she was about to get in, he leant over and gave her a quick kiss on the cheek. She nearly fell into the taxi. She was beginning to think that Damien let his guard down when he was drinking and perhaps that was why he was so careful about keeping his alcohol consumption under control.

It was business as usual the next morning in the office, and no mention was made of the previous evening. Over the next year Damien and Amanda had a few more "working dinners" but again, they were just that, and he always arranged for her transport home. On a few occasions other people from the department were invited and Amanda suspected this was to keep it above board and not raise suspicions about them being together too often.

She was becoming more and more attracted to Damien and found it increasingly difficult to keep her mind on her job when he was nearby. She had overheard a few calls from his wife, presumably about arrangements for that evening, but he was quite curt on the phone so it was difficult to gauge exactly what his marriage was like.

Amanda decided to tell Damien that she wanted a transfer, as she couldn't continue working with him feeling the way she did. She didn't want to do this in the office so suggested they go to the wine bar where they had celebrated her birthday. She just told him there was something she needed to discuss with him out of the office, and so he readily agreed that they go there that evening.

When they had been ushered into their usual booth and a glass of wine for each of them put on the table he said, "Okay, Amanda, what's the problem?" Amanda took a deep breath and told Damien that she couldn't continue working with him and was going to request a transfer. He looked absolutely dumfounded and asked her, "Why? What have I done?" She reassured him that it was nothing he had done but secretly thought it was more what he *hadn't* done that was making it difficult for her to work with him day by day. She decided to be honest about how she felt, no matter the consequences.

She said, "Damien, I can't work with you anymore because I am unable to maintain my professionalism while I have the feelings for you that I do." There, it was out in the open now and she felt better that she had been honest, but she wasn't prepared for his reply.

"Well thank goodness for that. I thought it was just me who felt that way." He gently took her hand in his "What are we going to do about it?"

Chapter 21

It was time for Caroline to check the contents of the red kettle, and to her delight she found that she had saved $1800. This was enough to buy an industrial-sized dough mixer, but the problem was where would she mix all this dough? She couldn't do it at home because Owen wasn't blind, and it would be too big to hide in a cupboard, which she had few of anyway. While talking it over with Margie in the coffee shop one day, a regular customer overheard and came across to speak with them.

Colleen owned the bottle shop next door, and her daughter Donna knew a woman who ran a business getting loans for fledgling enterprises and thought that Caromar Cookies might fit within the guidelines. Her business was originally started to help retrain stay-at-home mothers who wanted to rejoin the workforce with a home-based business and who had a great idea that needed financial backing. The friends just looked at each other in wonder and Margie asked, "Yes, that sounds great, what do we need to do?" Colleen said that she would phone their customer, Jennifer, and give her the number of the coffee shop so that she could make contact and see if she could help them.

The next afternoon Margie got a call from Jennifer, and they arranged to meet in two days when she was next in the area. Margie joked with her that she was at least guaranteed a good coffee and a tasty cookie for her trouble. Two days later, a nicely dressed young woman entered the coffee shop and asked for Margie. She introduced herself as Jennifer Simmons and handed them her business card. After the promised coffee and cookie, Jennifer assured them that the business would certainly meet the guidelines. They would be able to fit out a kitchen with equipment to expand the business and perhaps take on staff that was being retrained to return to the work force.

Arrangements were made that she would be back the same time tomorrow with all the information required for this government-funded scheme. Caroline and Margie gave each other a high five, decided it was definitely time for champagne, and went next door to give Colleen and Donna the good news.

Caroline was terrified of Owen finding out she was baking cookies at Margie's place but exhilarated that she may be able to make something of her life for her and Gavin. He was growing rapidly and wouldn't be having long sleeps and stay comfortable in the pram for much longer. There were a lot of issues to sort out, but she had never wanted anything so much in her life as for Caromar Cookies to grow and be a success. It was the only way she was going to extricate herself from Owen's control. She knew he was suspicious something was going on that he didn't know about and it wouldn't be long before he found out, one way or another.

Owen was home on Saturday, as usual reading the papers from cover to cover, and Caroline came in and announced that she was going to go for a walk to meet with a friend. "You don't have any friends except that horrible Margie," he retorted.

Caroline cheekily replied, "Well, that is one more friend than you have" and pushing the pram through the front door, slammed it behind her. Owen was not happy with this rebellious streak he had noticed in her and put it all down to her friendship with Margie. As per usual, he accepted no responsibility for what was happening to his marriage. It was much easier to just blame someone else.

Caroline had put a casserole in the oven for dinner before she left home, and when Margie closed the coffee shop at four it was time to put their heads together again and go over the forms that Jennifer had dropped in through the week. There was such a lot of information to go through that it would take hours so they decided to divide it up between them. Caroline knew she couldn't take the forms home, so decided to leave them with Margie and read them when she was at the coffee shop.

As Margie had the retail experience she would go through those sections and Caroline would look through the regulations for food preparation, handling, and storage. The financial side would be checked next time they could get together. Jennifer had informed them that they had thirty days to apply for the scheme but she would be calling in for her coffee as usual so if they had any questions she would be available. The three women had an instant rapport and felt that this was an idea that would get off the ground with everyone's effort and input.

When Caroline arrived back home later on Saturday afternoon, Owen just looked up from his paper and asked, "When's dinner?" She assured him it would be on the table in ten minutes as she had a casserole in the oven.

He just glared at her and said, "It had better be or there will be trouble." Exactly what sort of trouble was never specified, but he mistakenly thought the threat would be enough to keep Caroline in line. She turned on her heel and walked into the kitchen to put his precious dinner on the table but didn't dish hers up. She didn't want to sit across the table from him anymore and besides, Gavin needed feeding.

Caroline took Gavin into the bedroom to feed him as Owen had made it quite clear he didn't want to see "that child," as he referred to him, being fed in that disgusting manner. She was sure he was becoming even more unhinged than she had previously thought, especially when it came to the physical side of life but chose not to push the boundaries—just yet.

After Gavin was fed, changed, and settled in his cot, Caroline returned to the kitchen to eat her dinner. Owen's dirty plate and cutlery were just where he had left them, and he was nowhere to be seen. That was a bonus; she could have her dinner by herself and took it on a tray into the lounge to eat in front of the television. At least she could watch whatever she liked without him changing channels with the remote from one news broadcast to another.

Owen had appeared in the doorway and shouted "And don't think you are going to spill casserole all over my mother's lounge either." She tipped the plate up; it missed the lounge but decorated the rug occupying the middle of the floor. Owen was furious. He came over and raised his hand as though to hit her. She was very frightened but wasn't going to back down.

"If you touch me I will report you to the police, and let everyone at work know what a bully you are." It was the last statement rather than the former that got his attention, and he lowered his arm.

"Now clean up the mess," he instructed her.

Under her breath she said, "Well it's not as though you will rush to do it."

Caroline set the lounge room to rights, threw the rest of her dinner in the bin, and retreated to her bedroom where Gavin was sound asleep. She couldn't sleep because she was so excited about her discussion with Margie that afternoon. They could make a success of this—she just knew it. Women these days were cashed up but time poor, and who doesn't love the smell of freshly cooked biscuits straight from the oven? Real estate agents have this tactic in their arsenal of ways to help sell a home.

Her mind was whirling with ideas for new recipes, different flavours, maybe cut-out cookies for children, Christmas stars and bells, Easter bunnies—oh, the possibilities were endless. They just had to get started, and when Owen went to work on Monday she would sit in the coffee shop with the papers and do her part of the research as agreed with Margie. Gavin was growing and she could put him in the play area near her chair where he would be quite happy.

For this new venture to go ahead, she knew she would have to work out what to do with Gavin while she spent time mixing up cookie dough and trying out new recipes. She didn't want to put her darling baby into day care, but he was getting too big to be sleeping in the pram while she trundled cookies down to Margie and brought groceries back. She couldn't have someone come to the house in case Owen found out, although how that would happen she didn't know, as he never spoke to the neighbours, but best to err on the side of caution. He also didn't take any sick days or holidays because he thought he was so important that the company wouldn't survive his absence. She would ask Jennifer next time she saw her how other mothers managed, as they were the ones this scheme was trying to help. Maybe she could trade baby-sitting with another young mum who was in a similar situation.

She broached the subject to Margie next time she went to the coffee shop and was floored by her response. She was finding that spending all day in the shop was hard on her legs now. She had no family and had recently bought a small cottage not far from the shop. She suggested to Caroline that she could mind Gavin at her home and would look for a manager to run the shop. That way she would still have control of the business, and an income, but could help Caroline out by minding Gavin whom she looked on as her grandson. It seemed a marvellous solution, but there was even more to come.

"I think it would be a good idea if you baked the cookies at my home and that way you can set up the industrial mixer, which will make it faster and therefore more cookies can be made. You can cook them in my oven, or we will install a bigger one if we need it, and you can be with Gavin as well. What do you think?"

Caroline just looked at her and then burst into tears.

"I'm sorry, did I say something wrong?"

"No" said Caroline through her tears "You just said everything right. You will never know how grateful I am to you."

"We can talk about who pays for what and all that financial stuff once we get you sorted with Gavin. His welfare is the most important here, and he won't be looked after by strangers, just his mother and sort-of-grandma".

Some days were just filled with sunshine and hope, and this day had been one of them.

--o0o-

Chapter 22
Lindy

LINDY didn't think it was possible to be so bowed down by grief and still keep breathing. She had just come home after the funeral of her beloved husband of twenty-eight years. She sat in her favourite cushioned window seat, gazing out over their garden that John had lovingly tended until his dreadful diagnosis of inoperable cancer had been delivered just twelve months ago, and thought back over their life together.

Lindy and John had met in high school and started going out together when she was eighteen and he was twenty. They married three years later, much against her parent's advice as they thought she was too young, but for Lindy there was nowhere else she wanted to be but in John's arms as his wife.

Due to her parents' strong opposition, Lindy decided she would forego the big white spectacular in favour of a small wedding with just a few friends. If her parents wanted to attend, then it was up to them. All she wanted to do was to be the wife of the man she loved, and, if she had to do without an extravaganza with cars full of bickering bridesmaids, arguments over what colour dresses, flowers, hairdos, etc., then she would be missing nothing. She knew from cousins and girlfriends how the simple question "would you like to be my bridesmaid?" could turn a normal girl into a Bridezilla, capable of the most horrendous deeds just to show everyone for a day that she was special. Lindy knew she was special because John told her so every time they were together and that was good enough for her.

She took John with her when she chose her simple outfit for their wedding, because she wanted his opinion, although the final choice would be hers. Her mother, Muriel, was horrified "Can't you even think for yourself now?" Lindy just walked away and headed for the local coffee shop where she and John were going to go over their guest list, small though it was. They had booked a local restaurant, chosen a set menu and a drinks list, and now it was just a matter of writing out the invitations, then posting them off.

As it was likely they would have to pay for the wedding themselves, they erred on the side of restraint and kept the guest list to just twenty people, including Lindy's parents. It was therefore likely with the present atmosphere surrounding the event that there would only be eighteen people present, but so be it. She was determined that the presence or absence of her parents would not ruin her day—no matter what.

The day of John and Lindy's wedding dawned bright and sunny. They had already found a small flat and had moved in their meagre possessions. With some money they had been given by John's grandparents they had bought a bedroom suite and some lovely linen. They were so thrilled setting up their first home together that it didn't matter if they had mismatched second-hand china, inadequate cutlery, and hardly anything to cook with. They just wanted to be together, and by the end of the day their wish would be granted. They had decided to forego a honeymoon, mainly because of the cost, but promised themselves a great holiday on their first wedding anniversary.

The small chapel they had chosen had been decorated with flowers for the following day's church services and looked absolutely beautiful. Lindy's father walked his daughter down the aisle and handed her over to John when instructed by the minister. He then sat beside his stony-faced wife. She was still hanging onto the idea that Lindy was too young to get married but had quite forgotten that she had been only six months older when she had plighted her troth all those years ago. She would have had to be blind to not see the loving looks that passed between Lindy and John as they stood facing each other at the altar.

There was almost an incandescent glow around them that showed the whole world how much in love they were.

The service finished and the guests adjourned to the small courtyard adjacent to the church for photographs. It was then into the cars and off to the restaurant. In the short time it had taken for the service and photographs, someone had managed to tie tin cans and old boots to the back of John's car and write Just Married in toothpaste all across the back window.

The meal was beautiful, the speeches interspersed with anecdotes about them both, and hilarious laughter rang out throughout the celebration. It was a joyful day for Lindy and John, and they would remember it for the rest of their lives together and hoped they would have a long and happy marriage until they were old and grey.

Lindy continued with her office job until she was six months pregnant with their first child when she was twenty-three years old. Her pregnancy went wonderfully well and Lindy just glowed with good health. She didn't suffer morning sickness, swollen ankles, bad skin or any of the other possibilities she'd read about in her impending motherhood books, but she did get tired midafternoon. She relished taking a cool shower and having a quiet hour or two with the blinds drawn. Some afternoons she slept deeply, but most of the time she just dozed and wondered what her boy or girl would be like. Would he or she have curly fair hair like John, or long straight dark brown hair like her? She spent many hours imagining what this little person would want to do with their life when they grew up and hoped that they would have a happy healthy future.

Over the two years of her marriage Lindy had spent some time with her mother, who was gradually getting used to the idea that her daughter was a married woman, and she was overjoyed when she was told that she was going to be a grandma. That bit of news changed everything for the better. Nobody in a store was safe from being told that she had a grandchild on the way and she was doing a bit of shopping for it. Her mother had never been one to spend money very willingly, but the purse strings had been pulled wide open, and no baby store or department missed out on a purchase of some sort.

Lindy was mildly amused to think that her child needed so many tiny clothes, according to her mother, and the sheets for the bassinet and cot were piled up on a shelf ready to be used by this little being waiting in the wings. Bootees were knitted in white, lemon, blue, and pink with matching jackets, bonnets, and in some instances dresses. Her mother always seemed to have a garment suspended between the knitting needles and took it wherever she went, except church. "There is a limit," she was known to say.

As Lindy approached her due date, her mother started to suggest that she might move in for six or eight weeks after the birth "to help out." Lindy and John talked it over and felt it would be mean not to let her come and stay, even though Lindy knew it would be like living with an express train with the lever pulled way out. Her mother was not one to accept "No" as the end to a suggestion, and Lindy knew she would probably need some help, so a six-week time frame was agreed upon. She was doubtful that she would be able to get her mother to leave after the six weeks without some fairly positive persuasion, such as putting her bag in the car and driving her home. Time would tell.

Chapter 23

Lindy's due date finally arrived, but she went just a few days over before Baby No. 1 decided to make his entrance into the world. John wasn't allowed into the ward but was one of the pacing, coffee-drinking about-to-be-dads in the maternity waiting room. Even though uncomfortable-looking chairs were provided, along with years-old magazines, the thing to do seemed to be to pace, go outside for a smoke, or lean against the wall with eyes fixed on the big plastic swing doors. Sooner or later, preferably sooner, your name would be called and the remaining population of the maternity waiting room would slap the chosen guy on the back and wish him "good luck."

As the hours went by, males disappeared through the swing doors and others came in to wait. It was a transient club of males who wanted to be the next to have their name called so they could go and see what their wife had managed to produce. It was not the "done thing" in the 70s for men to be with their wives and they were kept firmly out of the way until the deed was done and their wife was all prettied up for the inspection of the new offspring.

It didn't matter if their experience had been horrendous, painful, and something they hoped they didn't have to go through again; it was necessary for them to look as though they had been for a gentle stroll in the park and just happened to find a baby to bring back with them. It was all nonsense really, and it was no wonder men really had no idea what went on to produce their child. It also wasn't nice to go into the gory details so there was a lot of smoke and mirrors about how the child actually got here.

Lindy and John now had a baby son they decided to call Scott, and John for his second name. He was a red-faced bundle with a mop of dark curly hair that was still damp from his post-birth wipe-down. He was not very happy about being installed in a fluorescent-lit room, tightly wrapped in a hospital rug so no hands could emerge, and made his displeasure evident by crying in a very loud voice for an eight-pound baby boy.

Lindy was holding him in her arms when John walked into the room, and he thought he had never seen anything so beautiful as his beloved wife with his son. His throat choked up, and as he bent down to kiss Lindy on the cheek, a little hand popped out of the rug and touched John's chin. John's eyes filled with tears at the sight of the little being that the love between him and Lindy had created, and he fell in love with his son. That love at the start of Scott's life would be just as strong when John took his last breath just over two decades later.

They were a happy, healthy trio when they left the hospital a few days later and Lindy was installed in her own home. Her mother had, of course, come over and staked her claim as soon as she heard Lindy had gone to hospital to have Scott. She was quick to point out that she didn't like Scott as a first name, but John was alright for a second name, but she would have preferred something else less modern, like George or Albert. Lindy and John just looked at each other and laughed. All was right with the world as Lindy's mother was complaining, which was no less than they had expected. She never had learned to just roll with the punches, as the saying goes. Her thinking was more "my way or the highway" but in this case she didn't have a say, which no doubt was a new experience for her.

Over the course of the next few weeks a routine of sorts was established for Lindy and Scott. Endless advice was received from Muriel, some of which was accepted but almost as much was rejected. It was starting to feel like a long six weeks to Lindy, but it was nice to have her mother make a cup of tea or cook the evening meal for them so John could have a decent dinner when he returned home from work. Lindy and Muriel had some quiet times together too and spent a lot of time just gazing at Scott as he slept, which fortunately he did for the majority of the day. He was a contented baby for the most part and was only vocal when something was wrong in his world such as a dirty nappy or a hungry tummy.

He was a delightful baby, and his bassinet was the first place John headed for every evening, straight after he hugged and kissed Scott's mother and enquired about how her day had gone. He really only half listened to the answers because he was already on his way down the hallway in search of his son and heir. Lindy could quite understand the attraction because she felt the same way. She knew that their lives would never be the same again, now that this little person was the centre of their universe.

After eight weeks, and with almost hourly hints that she should go home, Muriel left her beloved grandson behind and reluctantly returned to her somewhat quiet existence. She hadn't realised how special being a grandparent could be and bored her friends almost rigid with tales of every dribble and noise that her amazing, talented, clever, and quite delightful grandson contributed to her world in a day.

Her very best friend eventually gently told her that while they were delighted she had such a marvellous addition to her family, they would actually like the old Muriel back. Yes, they admitted they were interested to hear about Scott's latest adventure or milestone achieved, but really could she please talk about something else as well, or preferably instead of Scott? Muriel took the thinly veiled hint that she had become a boring person talking ad nauseum about her grandson and left him out of every second conversation. That was the best she could do so they would just have to put up with it. As usual, it was her way or the highway. Some things never change.

Chapter 24

Scott grew into a happy, contented toddler and when he was two years six months old a sister was added to the family. Ruby had blond fine silky hair that floated around her head like a windblown halo, above two startling blue eyes. Even when she was older clips never seemed to keep her hair tamed as they just slid out, plaits came undone with the slightest bit of activity, and she just never looked tidy. No matter what was done to Ruby's hair, it had a way of undoing what had just been done in a remarkably short time.

Ruby was a rebel. As she and Scott grew she became the leader of all sorts of mischief. She learned to climb trees at a very young age, almost straight after she could walk, and would often be found a terrifying height from the ground. She was fearless, impatient, intelligent, and the most delightful child—on a good day. A Ruby Bad Day was not something anyone enjoyed. She could throw a temper tantrum like no other child Lindy or John had ever had the misfortune to come in contact with.

She could coerce her brother into anything as he was her willing slave and was in awe of her displeasure if he didn't do what she wanted, and immediately. But in spite of all this, they were the best of friends and would look after each other no matter what the situation. As they grew older they each had their own friends but would never let the other one down. They would rather change their arrangements than disappoint their sibling and this attitude lost them some friends along the way. It didn't worry either of them because they always had each other.

Lindy was a conservative parent, and Ruby was very spirited, so this caused some friction between the two females in the household. Lindy liked things done the right way, as she had been taught to do. She liked a neat, clean, and well-cared-for home: meals on the table at a certain time each evening and for the family to all sit down together and discuss their day over dinner. Ruby, however, couldn't care less about the right way; mess was best, and dinnertime was the right hour of the day for talking to friends on the phone. She was uninterested in how many clients her dad had seen that day and how much they had contributed to the company, blah, blah, blah.

It was a constant battle on Lindy's part to try to impose some order at the end of the day and to get Ruby to fit in with the family routine. The shouting on Ruby's part was loud and often, usually with the phrase "I don't want to" in there somewhere. By the time she was sixteen, Lindy had learned that she had to choose her battles with the rebellious teenager and gave in to a certain extent on some issues. She just shut the door on Ruby's room when it was unfit for human habitation. Lindy hoped that one day her daughter might change, but she also knew that was about as likely as her being crowned Mrs World.

Lindy loved her dearly. She didn't understand her, but then again nobody in the household did with the possible exception of Scott, who seemed to be able to work out what was going on in Ruby World. If Lindy wanted Ruby to do something in particular that was important to the family, she asked Scott if he could convince his sister to go along with it, just this once. Sometimes he succeeded and other times it was a definite "No way. You can stuff that idea, brother dear."

Lindy and John's love affair survived their two children, and they duly celebrated their twenty-fifth wedding anniversary. They invited everyone who had been at their wedding, with the exception of Muriel, who had passed away quietly one night in her sleep ten years before. The celebration was held at home and Ruby, for once, helped out with the food and drinks without so much as a complaint. Scott thought she must have been unknowingly put on some medication to adjust her mood swings and make her what he called normal.

Scott was twenty-three years old, and Ruby was coming up twenty-one. She refused point blank a twenty-first birthday celebration that would probably be full of old people—her definition of anyone over forty—and declared that she would rather go canyoning, parachuting over the mountains, or white water rafting. Predictably, her mother was horrified at all this death defying recreation, but then again Ruby had fallen out of a tree before she was three years old and survived that.

Scott opted out as he was much less danger loving than his sister, and when he was twenty-one years old he had taken the option of a nice cheque to put towards a car he had his eye on. His sister had declared it was a boring choice and he should live on the edge a little. Lindy made the comment that one daredevil in the family was enough for any mother thank you very much, but she did agree to drive Ruby to the airport for whatever destination she chose. Lindy decided that after she dropped her off she would then go home and have a stiff drink, or however many it took to get her to be able to sleep until Ruby returned home, indefinite though that was.

It never ceased to amaze her that two conservative adults such as she and John had managed to produce this whirlwind child who took the world by the tail and shook the hell out of it. She was perpetual motion, full of ideas that no one else had even thought of, and could charm the birds out of the trees, provided she wasn't up in one at the time. She sent money to charities trying to save some endangered species in a country nobody could spell let alone identify on a map. She would see a homeless person and take them to the closest McDonald's for a meal. A bedraggled kitten would be given a home on the quilt in Ruby's room, and it could be a few days before anyone knew it was there. She loved life, and she was going to cram as much into it as she could for as long as possible.

Over a few weeks John came home from work and often complained that he was tired and just didn't feel well. It was nothing specific, but Lindy knew it was not like him to complain of ill health and she suggested he visit their doctor. Blood tests were done, x-rays and ultrasounds, and the awful diagnosis delivered a week later. John had cancer. The bottom fell out of their world with those few words and they just looked at each other in shock.

"How long do I have, Doctor?"

"We can help with some chemo and radiation, but it is throughout your body, and I think you will probably have a year at the most." The doctor made an initial appointment for John to go and see an oncologist and discuss his options.

Neither of them was capable of driving the short distance home, so they found a quiet coffee shop and sat there thinking their own thoughts until their coffee went cold and their cookies left untouched. They left, and Lindy drove home, trying very hard to keep her mind on what she was doing so they didn't have an accident.

They were both shocked into silence, but eventually they found each other and hugged so hard Lindy thought her bones would break. John was crying, she was crying, and they realised that their children would have to be told. John's terminal illness was going to affect the whole family, and Lindy wanted their children to know as soon as possible.

It was a terrible afternoon for them both and they alternated between hugging each other, crying, and trying to eat or drink something just to keep going and also to have some focus other than the word CANCER that had just been added to their family vocabulary. Scott arrived home from work at his usual time and Ruby was not far behind, having spent the day rattling a tin in the city to raise money for another of her causes.

"Mum and I have something to tell you. Please come and sit down." Their children looked at each other, Scott with raised eyebrows and Ruby with a theatrical shrug of her shoulders. John then told them what had transpired at the doctor's surgery that day and the prognosis he had been given. Lindy sat beside John with her head bowed and tears running down her face, which she mopped at with a hankie. Her children had never seen her cry and were absolutely silent. They didn't know it then, but Lindy crying was going to be something they would see again and again as their dad's illness progressed.

--oOo--

Chapter 25

Amanda was no longer working with Damien, but they could not deny their feelings for each other, and the attraction was very strong on both their parts. He told her that he had been married for ten years but regretted his choice of wife. She was a good mother to their two boys but was certainly not a corporate wife. She point blank refused to go to any dinners, conferences, or anything associated with the company. According to Damien the boys were her priority, and he was just the breadwinner.

He informed Amanda that he and his wife had separate bedrooms, as he often got home late and rose early to go back to the office. She didn't like being disturbed late at night, and he often got the boys up in the morning, gave them breakfast, and left them watching television before he went to work. He obviously adored his boys, but she wasn't quite sure what the situation was with his wife, even though Damien assured her that sex was off the agenda and had been for quite a while.

Amanda was not sure if he worked hard to be the breadwinner or whether he didn't want to go home, even if he did have two sons. It was hard to know if Damien was telling the whole truth or whether he was telling her what he thought she would want to hear. It was not the first time he had had a relationship outside his marriage, but he wasn't about to tell Amanda that snippet of information. This was actually the reason he had been transferred to this department and he had been promised confidentiality.

Over the next six months Amanda tried very hard to not get involved with Damien. She realised she was getting older and hadn't yet managed to find a man she could settle down with and have a family. She was a career girl but mostly due to the absence of any other choices. She did not like the idea of being "the other woman," even if Damien and his wife were not sleeping together. It caused her many nights of tossing and turning in her lonely bed.

Their professional paths didn't cross very often, but when they did it was like a crackle of electricity between them. Just an "accidental" brushing of hands was enough to give Amanda another sleepless night and more thoughts of *what am I going to do?* She had never been faced with this sort of problem before and had no close girlfriends to talk it over with. From what she could see of the other single women in the company their motto was "If you want it, go get it."

Damien asked Amanda if she would have dinner with him as, in his words, "This is killing me not being able to be with you." Amanda knew she was playing with fire and may be putting her feet on a path that would lead to personal and professional disaster, but agreed to go out that night. He named a restaurant they hadn't been to before and asked Amanda to get a taxi there, and he would meet her at seven.

She didn't have time to go home and change so did the best she could in the ladies room with the contents of her desk drawer where she kept make-up, a few pieces of costume jewellery, and a pair of killer heels—only to be worn from the kerb to the table and then elegantly displayed while sitting down. She called them her S & P shoes (sit and pose).

Damien had already arrived when Amanda alighted from the taxi and she was shown to the table. He had an ice bucket with champagne chilling. She wasn't sure if, by the end of the evening, this would be a celebration or a commiseration. She was still mixed in her feelings of embarking on an affair with a married man.

They ordered dinner and talked about safe subjects until their entrée arrived. After these plates were cleared away, Damien took Amanda's hand and asked, "What are we going to do, my darling?"

She was rather taken aback by the "darling" bit but took it as a sign that he felt as strongly about her as she did about him.

Damien had not informed her that he often stayed in a city apartment provided by the company, for the use of executives if it was too late to go home to the 'burbs. Over the main meal he suggested that this could be their love nest but asked Amanda to not leave any of her belongings in the apartment just in case other executives used it at any time. This struck a sour note for her. *Is it our love nest or just a convenient place to have sex?* This would need sorting out and the sooner the better. It had not escaped Damien's attention that Amanda had suddenly gone quiet and didn't seem as though she wanted to go along with his plan of using the city apartment so he tried another tack.

"You don't seem to want to use the company apartment. Would you prefer we go to your place instead?" This didn't sit well with her either but it was the better option. She lived in a very big building where neighbours hardly saw each other more than once a week and that was usually in the elevator morning or evening. It was a rather anonymous existence but for a love affair it was perfect. Amanda still couldn't quite believe that she was actually making plans to be with a married man in a sexual relationship. There was one person who must not know and that was her mother.

Amanda had never been in this situation before—on many levels. She had broken her own rule of not dating anyone in the company, especially the boss, she was contemplating going ahead with an affair with a married man, and should he have a key? There were so many unanswered questions but her feelings for Damien couldn't be denied. She was not her usual levelheaded self and hadn't even thought about where this could take her.

If she embarked on this affair, would Damien get a divorce? She doubted this would be an option, as he had never even mentioned leaving his wife and children. Was she giving up her chance of having a husband and family? Probably, but what was her alternative? Deny her feelings and stay single until a more promising male came along or just jump in the deep end and hope for the best?

Amanda was heading towards thirty, and her biological clock was making loud ticking noises. She spent hours while sleepless in her bed at home thinking about whether she should have a child and bring it up by herself. She loved Damien but wasn't sure he would ever divorce his wife, and even if he did, he already had two boys and Amanda wasn't sure she could cope with a blended family. It might look okay on television, but in real life?

She came to the momentous decision that she would have Damien's baby but would not tell him about her pregnancy, if she were lucky enough to conceive. The plan was made, and she threw her contraceptive pills in the garbage. Damien came to Amanda's apartment at least once or twice a week and Amanda decided to let the universe look after this one.

Within eight weeks she was pregnant and had mixed feelings of joy and fear. She was joyful to be pregnant but fearful of what Damien would say, if she decided to tell him, as she had not discussed with him her desire to have a child. Would he want to be part of the child's life? Would he want her to abort his son or daughter? Amanda knew she would have to tell him but sensed that he would be very angry that he had been tricked, as he thought she was taking care of contraception. Time was on her side to work this out so she decided to just wait before telling Damien, if indeed that was her decision.

Amanda and Damien were due to go to a company dinner that night, and they had previously discussed that they would come back to her apartment afterwards, in separate taxis of course. There was still an element of cloak and dagger to their relationship, and he wanted to keep their affair under wraps and not let anyone in the company know.

It had been his decision to keep his love affair a secret, not so much because of the company he worked for, but because he actually had quite a healthy marriage with his wife and she was pregnant with their third child – even though he had told Amanda that they were not sleeping together.

Amanda walked into the ballroom where the dinner was being held. And the first two people she saw were Damien and his obviously pregnant wife. He was looking after her like she was a piece of Dresden china. Amanda almost collapsed and could not believe her eyes but before Damien even knew she was in the room, she had fled through the front doors of the hotel and tearfully asked for a taxi to her apartment. The doorman was quite concerned and asked her if she was all right and if there was anything he could do for her. She just shook her head and climbed into the taxi, giving the driver her address.

When she got home she was so distressed that she fell on the bed, still fully clothed, and only just managed to kick her shoes off. She couldn't believe that her lover had so obviously lied about his relationship with his wife. Amanda was distraught but her underlying resilience came to the fore and at midnight she got up to have a cup of coffee. She couldn't sleep so while she was drinking her coffee she examined her options.

Tell Damien? Well it was obvious he wasn't going to leave his wife now there was Baby Three on the way, and he would be angry that he had been tricked into his lover having a child by deception. Bring up the child herself? That seemed to be her future. Her mother had done it, and she had survived, but it would mean leaving her job and going somewhere out of the city.

She doubted Damien would actually come looking for her. This knowledge added to her sadness, but after all, she had always known he was married, and she was the one who had let him stay at her apartment when it suited them both. In about seven months she was going to have the proof of that in her arms. It was time to decide what to do with the rest of her life now that she had a child to consider.

--oOo--

Chapter 26

After dinner, another meal for which she neither expected nor received thanks, Owen said, "When you have finished your chores, you had better sit down. I have something to say to you." She tidied the kitchen and made a cup of tea to take to the table and sat opposite her husband. From his demeanour it was obvious he was displeased about something, which was not unusual.

"What did you want to talk to me about as you don't even speak to me at home?"

He announced, "I have telephoned home through the day, at various times, and you haven't been here. Where have you been?"

"Have you been spying on me? If you have, you would know where I have been, and there is nothing you can do about it. If you hadn't kept me short of money I wouldn't need to do what I did."

Owen was floored by her reply and, with his sexual hang-ups, he immediately thought she had been prostituting herself around the neighbourhood. When he told her his suspicion, she just burst out laughing.

"You have cured me of wanting anything to do with men, thank you very much, and for your information I have been making cookies to earn a bit of money."

Owen just looked at her with a stunned expression on his face. Caroline took a deep breath and then continued to tell him that she was tired of him always calling the shots and that she'd had enough of his behaviour. By this time, Owen had collapsed onto one of the kitchen chairs and was hanging onto the edge of the table as though he would fall to the floor if he didn't keep his grip. He was white around the mouth from anger, and his normally pale eyes were glittering with rage.

He spluttered and stammered, which amused Caroline, because Owen was usually so well controlled. He finally gained control and yelled at her, "And whose money have you been using?"

Caroline took the greatest joy in calmly answering, "Well, to start with it was yours, but now it is mine." This was all a bit too much for Owen, and he raised his hand as though he was going to hit Caroline but then thought better of it after seeing the defiant look in her eyes.

Caroline had tasted financial freedom and very much liked the flavour. She continued to tell him that he should be more responsible for himself and not expect her to do everything for him as she had enough to do looking after Gavin and earning a bit of money. Owen was shocked into silence but only temporarily.

His response was typical of him, and he accused her of doing everything for "your brat" and neglecting her husband but ignored the fact that he was an adult and Gavin a toddler. Owen rose from the chair with a furious look on his face. He pointed towards the front door and told Caroline, "Get out of my house and go live with your revolting friend Margie." whom Owen thought was largely to blame for this obstinate streak that his wife had developed. He didn't realise that he had just given Caroline everything she had been working for—freedom.

Caroline put Gavin in the pram, although he was almost too big now, and packed as many of his things as possible into the bag on the back. She then packed a suitcase for herself with what she needed for a day or so. She planned to come back when Owen was at work to get the rest of her things. She was off to Margie's where she knew she would be welcome, and safe from her husband's rages. In the background Owen was ranting and raving about what an ungrateful bitch she had become since she had known that old bag down at the coffee shop. He was still enraged when she slammed the front door behind her and went out into the cold starry night.

Thank you Owen. Freedom here I come.

She walked the short distance to Margie's home and knocked on the front door. A minute or so went by and then the one person in the world that Caroline most wanted to be with, except for her son of course, opened the door. Margie was lost for words when she saw Caroline standing behind the pram on her front veranda, laden down with a suitcase and backpack. It didn't take her long to regain her composure, and she held the door wide while Caroline and Gavin proceeded down the hall to Margie's beautiful lounge area.

"What has happened? Are you alright?" Margie asked while settling Caroline down on the lounge and extricating Gavin from his warm nest in the pram. He threw his arms around Margie's neck and gave her a big kiss on the cheek. "Hello, Gamma," he said in his sleepy voice. He was such a loving little boy and so happy when he was with his mum and Gamma. He had never been able to get his tongue around the traditional title of Grandma so invented his own title for this loving older lady who took such good care of him.

Over a welcome glass of wine Caroline told Margie what had transpired with Owen and how she didn't need telling twice to leave. She was planning to go back the next day when Owen was at work and get some more of her belongings, but she would never sleep another night in the house with that wretched man. She didn't realise just how prophetic her statement was.

The flat above the shop had been empty since Margie and Prince moved into her own home so she offered it to Caroline as a safe haven until she could get herself organised. Once again Margie had come to Caroline's rescue. Caroline and Margie settled down for the night, and the plan was for Caroline to go to the flat above the shop the next day, with their meagre belongings. Once that was done, she planned to return to the house to retrieve the rest of her things while Margie looked after Gavin.

The morning dawned bright and shiny and truly reflected the way Caroline felt. It had been a long time since she'd slept so well and woke refreshed and ready to face whatever the day brought, even if it might include running into Owen. He now didn't know what to expect from Caroline's behaviour, but she was sure he would be mulling over her answer about having used "his" money before and, now, "my own."

As soon as breakfast was over, Caroline rang the local solicitor she had used for the sale of her parents' house to seek advice about her position now that her husband had effectively told her he didn't want her in "his" house again. She was hoping that this was the beginning of a legal separation, and she could get on with her life without being harassed by this man she married not that long ago.

She had glimpsed how good life could be when you had a few dollars in your pocket, earned with your own hands, and could decide what to do with it. She momentarily felt guilty that she had hidden this enterprise from Owen, but at the same time she knew she had to do something or she would be stuck with him forever, and that was a future she was doing her best to avoid.

Margie offered to mind Gavin so Caroline could go to the solicitor and work out what her options were. She knew that she would have a fight on her hands with getting any money out of Owen. Paying any money to Caroline for the brat was not high on his list of priorities, and he would do almost anything to get out of it. The law, however, may have a different idea as to child support and these were the things that Caroline needed to find out. She made an appointment to go and see her solicitor the next day.

The solicitor gave her plenty of information about her rights and what she could expect to receive from Owen in child support. Caroline didn't tell the solicitor Owen's views on anything to do with paying money for his son. The solicitor would find out soon enough when Owen received a letter bringing him up to speed with the law. Caroline wanted to be fair with Owen but suspected that he would not reciprocate.

Mostly what Caroline wanted was to retrieve the money that was taken from her when she married Owen, in the form of the balance of the sale of her parents' house and the forced sale of Betty. She'd consider anything else she'd be awarded a bonus. She realised that she had been young and naïve, but because her parents had such a sharing marriage she assumed everyone did.

Caroline returned to Margie's place later that afternoon, and they discussed the information the solicitor has provided her with. She intended to go back that night and tell Owen she wanted a divorce, but Margie warned her to be careful as she was afraid how he would react when it came down to paying out any money. In effect, Owen and Caroline had been separated but living under the same roof since before Gavin was born. Margie asked Caroline to not discuss anything other than a separation at this point because, if divorce and child support was mentioned, she knew that would send Owen into a fury and perhaps endanger Caroline's safety.

After dinner, with Gavin tucked up in bed at Margie's place, Caroline borrowed Margie's car and drove the short distance to Owen's place. She had never really thought of it as her home and used her key to enter. Unexpectedly, she met Owen as he came up the hallway with a furious look on his face.

"What do you think you are doing? You are breaking into my home!"

"I just want to talk to you," Caroline replied in a calm voice. Owen turned on his heel and strode off down the hallway towards the kitchen, while shouting over his shoulder, "Well, I don't want to talk to you. As far as I'm concerned you are dead to me, and while you are here you can leave the keys behind, and I don't want you in my house ever again."

Caroline had expected some resistance, but this was getting ridiculous. When Owen turned around she was a little taken aback by the look of pure hatred on his face and the manic glitter in his eyes. The thought crossed her mind that he might have been drinking, but then again he would never pay for alcohol, so that wasn't a possibility. She tried talking to him, but he just shouted back at her, so after a few minutes of this behaviour Caroline decided she wasn't going to get anywhere with him and walked up the hallway to the front door.

She wasn't intending to leave her keys with him because her belongings were still in the house, but just as she reached the front door Owen put his arm around her throat and snatched the keys out of her hand. Caroline was becoming quite frightened and just as she opened the door to the front veranda, he gave her a hard push in the back that almost sent her stumbling down the steps. As she regained her balance the front door slammed behind her but not before Owen had declared, "You won't get anything out of me, you bitch."

She was shaking when she got to the car and slowly drove back to Margie's place. She suspected he had become more mentally unstable so she would just stay away from him and communicate through her solicitor. Owen didn't know that Caroline had long ago given Margie a front door key, just in case she ever lost hers. She would need it tomorrow when she went to collect the rest of her belongings.

Early the next morning Caroline was woken by fire engines roaring up the street but didn't take much notice, even though sirens were unusual here. They stopped not far away, and Caroline was curious about where the fire was but certainly didn't expect it to be just up the road at her previous address.

When she arrived outside the front fence she could see that there was a pile of clothes alight in the middle of the lawn, and Owen was throwing more stuff on top. Caroline realised with horror that it was actually her belongings and Gavin's that were being thrown onto the pile. Through the haze of smoke she could see Owen and saw that he had a gleeful expression on his face, an expression she had never witnessed before, and he was jumping up and down with what looked like excitement every time he threw something else on the increasing flames.

The fire engine crew had arrived and were rolling out the hoses to hook up to the pump, but by then the pile of Caroline's worldly goods was rapidly being reduced to a pile of ashes. She just looked on in shock, but then regained her composure and ran to where Owen was standing. He had stopped jumping up and down as he had exhausted his supply of things to burn.

Caroline grabbed him by the shoulder and spun him around to face her. "What do you think you are doing?" she cried out in an anguished voice.

"I told you you wouldn't get anything out of me!" he screamed back in her face. "I have wiped you out of my life, and you won't need to ever come back here again. There is nothing of yours left. I made a special point of burning that revolting red kettle, and it will never hold water again," he shouted at her.

Caroline had to try hard to keep the smile off her face as she thought of what the red kettle had actually held, and it had not been water. The red kettle had been the container for her money and therefore her freedom. She was sad to see it go, but it had more than served her purpose. The money was safe in a bank account in Caroline's name but at Margie's address.

The fire crew could see there was a domestic dispute going on and had called the police, who arrived only a few minutes later. The male police officer then tried to take Owen by the arm to move him away from Caroline, but Owen looked as though he was beyond all reason by then and started screaming at the officer, "I told the bitch she wouldn't get anything, and I have burned everything she ever brought to my house."

By this time the female officer had taken a crying and shocked Caroline aside and asked her what had happened. She was appalled by her story, and had already decided that Owen looked as though he was quite mad, or at the very least out of control. She was going to recommend that a psychiatrist assess him as his behaviour was definitely way outside the square of normal.

Owen was trying to shake off the officer, but after a minute or so he found himself firmly gripped by a set of handcuffs and unceremoniously dumped into the back of the police wagon. Caroline was asked to come down to the station as soon as possible and make a statement about what had happened. She explained to the officers that she had a small child to look after but would come down once she organised someone to do this for her.

As she passed the pile of smouldering ashes in the middle of the lawn, she wondered if anything of hers had been missed in the house, but she doubted it. Owen would have thoroughly checked in every nook and cranny to find each item that Caroline had ever owned and treasured. He would not have cared that these bits and pieces of her past life actually meant something to her; they would just have been things he wanted destroyed because he knew it would affect her at her deepest level. She had the strange thought that poor Hurry got cremated twice.

However, Owen had underestimated the steely resolve that Caroline had acquired over the years and particularly since she had become a mother. She would go to the police station, and she would give an honest statement, including the fact that he took her car without her permission and sold it by forging her signature, the profits of which he squirreled away in an unknown bank account.

Betty, her beautiful new blue car, had been her chance of motorised freedom and Owen had stolen that away. She vowed that when he was back in the community again, whenever that might be, she would make sure she got that money back. She had somewhere to live now where she and Gavin were safe and would never be afraid of him again.

--o0o--

Chapter 27

Lindy's children, Scott and Ruby, had gotten on with their lives a year after John's death. She was very disenchanted with her existence, and it felt exactly like that—an existence, not a life. Her friends had gone back to whatever they had been doing before she became a widow, and Lindy realised that now all the necessary financial adjustments had been made, property title transferred, etc., she was really quite lonely.

She was not being invited to outings where she would be the odd woman out, even though these people had been their friends for years. She felt very much out of the social scene and struggled with being a single woman again.

She also realised that she would have to get a job to finish paying off the rather modest mortgage that remained on their home. Scott still lived at home, but like most young people, he didn't think everyday living should cost him anything other than personal expenses. Lindy had a long talk with him, and they came up with a plan for a joint pooling of resources. Predictably, Scott wasn't happy about it, but as he worked in finance he was well aware that he couldn't do better than living at home.

Ruby was quite another matter altogether. Her plan of attack to avoid responsibility for any contribution to the household was to yell and shout that she was hardly there anyway and why should she have to put in anything when she never had to before. "I can live cheaper overseas," she countered, and Lindy was so tempted to tell Ruby that maybe she should do just that. However, she decided to err on the side of caution, as she didn't want to lose her daughter to some God-forsaken place on the other side of the world. After a few more conversations about the R word, responsibility, Ruby grudgingly agreed to pay an amount per day when she was actually in the house. It was the best deal Lindy could come up with, and it was better than nothing.

It was time for Lindy to go back to work, and after several unsuccessful interviews she realised that experience was what she lacked, and she couldn't get experience without a job. She mentioned this difficulty to one of her neighbours, who advised her to source out a retraining course for women that would probably suit her quite well. Her contact person was Jennifer Simmons, and she arranged to meet up with Lindy the next Monday when she was in the area. The two women got along famously and as Jennifer was divorced she understood what it was like to be a single woman and totally responsible for earning a living.

While Jennifer was filling in the necessary forms, she was somewhat startled when Lindy admitted she hadn't worked since she married at twenty-one and had two children by the time she was twenty-five. Jennifer commented that with her excellent grooming and pleasant demeanour she didn't think Lindy would have any problems getting a job, after some retraining. After an hour or so, and several coffees, Jennifer asked Lindy what she would like to do so that the appropriate training would be organised. Jennifer asked Lindy to sleep on it overnight, and they would get together the next day.

After a lot of thought that evening, Lindy decided that she would like to work where she had a lot of public contact and the chance to learn new skills. She had run the school canteen for years, which required ordering supplies, budgeting, and most importantly, making a profit for the school. Although she had limited computer skills and really only knew how to email, go on Facebook, or source out information on where to buy something, she was willing to give anything a go.

Lindy enrolled in a small business management course but still needed to work part time to survive. Scott would probably contribute the agreed amount to the household but Ruby was as unreliable as the weather. It was more than likely that any money the girl managed to earn would be spent on food for some animal she had brought home rather than food for Lindy's pantry.

As part of her brief it was up to Jennifer to source out businesses that needed part-time staff, and she now thought Lindy would fit the bill perfectly. She was friendly, well groomed, willing to try anything, and most of all wanted to work. Margie had not had much success with younger employees as they were usually to be found out the back, talking on their mobile phone, checking emails, or looking at the latest You Tube video that they just couldn't resist.

Jennifer arranged for Margie and Lindy to meet after the café had closed for the day so they could talk in peace and quiet. The two women formed an immediate bond, and Margie could see that when Lindy had finished her course she would be a real asset to the business and agreed to take her on part time with the promise of a management role when she had finished her course.

Lindy struggled a bit at first with working and studying, as well as running her household, but she knew this was the doorway to a new life and income for her. Jennifer, as her mentor, reassured Lindy that she would be there for any problems that may arise. Lindy wished she could hand Ruby over to Jennifer at the moment as she had just come back from some animal welfare mission and was driving her mother crazy. There were posters all over the dining room table, and Ruby was constantly on her mobile trying to organise people for a protest march.

Margie was delighted with Lindy's performance in the coffee shop, and it was not long before she offered a pay rise. The profits of the shop were increasing, and Lindy had certainly been part of that with her pleasant manner and willingness to go that extra mile for a customer. She handled difficult people with a smile and seemed to be in ten places at once when the shop was busy.

As part of her new management role, and building on the skills she learned in her business management course, Lindy had a noticeboard on one wall of the shop where people could place flyers or advertisements. One Saturday morning, during a very busy period, a man came into the shop and introduced himself as Brian. He asked if he could see the manager and was directed to speak with Lindy as he wanted permission to put flyers on the noticeboard about new art classes that were starting up in the next school term. He quickly explained that they were trying to get people to join who were no longer teenagers but who lived alone or just wanted the chance to renew a long-forgotten dream and maybe make some new friends.

Lindy explained "I am really busy at the moment, but if you could come back after the lunch trade I would be happy to sit and talk with you." Art was something she didn't have time for when the children were little but would certainly be interested in trying again. Brian bought a coffee and snack but didn't get another chance to talk to Lindy. He was quite taken by the way she was so competent and pleasant to people, and he also realised that he rather liked the way she looked.

Brian had been widowed two years earlier when his wife died of breast cancer and he, like Lindy, was lonely and trying to find something to do with his life. His daughter and her family lived interstate, so he didn't get to see them very often and realised he couldn't rely on them for company. Most of his friends had gotten on with their lives and, apart from the occasional invitation to dinner, usually by a well-meaning friend who also provided a single woman for his company; he was quite alone for much of the time. He realised that he needed to reinvent his own life, and that was why he chose to distribute flyers around the town, in the hope of getting some other people to join the art classes.

Next time Brian went into the shop he chose a Monday afternoon, when the shop was not so busy, and was dismayed to see that Lindy was not there. On enquiring he was told that she was at the bank and would be back soon so he ordered a coffee and waited for her to return. About fifteen minutes later Lindy came back to the shop, recognised Brian, and gave him a wave. She put her bag down, poured herself a coffee, and said to the other assistant that she would just have a break for a few minutes.

She took her coffee over to where Brian was sitting and asked if he'd had had any response to the flyer he put up in the shop. As she sipped her coffee he replied that they'd had a few enquiries, and interest seemed to be building.

Lindy told him "I wouldn't mind trying art again. I used to love the freedom of sloshing paint on a board and I would lose myself for hours in what I was creating." Lindy explained that she hadn't painted since high school, as it was put on the back burner when she had her children, but it was something she thought would fill in a few very pleasant hours. Brian assured her "We have a nice bunch of people, all ages and range of talent. They just like to paint. It is more about having company and a shared interest."

Lindy started art classes and found out more about Brian's background. He told her that he had a small transport company but he'd sold it when his wife became ill and he then became her full-time caregiver. Lindy could relate to this as she had nursed her sick husband until his death too and knew what a toll it could take.

After his wife's death, Brian realised that the family home was far too big for him to rattle around in by himself and looked for something more compact. He had found a small cottage with a tiny garden that was enough for him to look after but would not consume every spare minute of his day. Brian sometimes did a shift driving for the company if they needed him, but most of the time he spent painting, doing some gardening, and was really at a loose end for a lot of hours per week.

He continued to come into the shop once or twice a week, and sometimes Lindy took a break to sit and chat with him. They never seemed to run out of things to say to each other, but Lindy was mindful that she was the manager and was there to work, not socialise for hours. She didn't want to give the other employees a bad example to follow, but every time she saw Brian she liked him even more.

Margie met Brian on one of her rare visits to the shop, and she liked him on sight. In a quiet moment she told Lindy "Brian seems a nice man and you have so much in common. Don't let him get away." and laughing retreated to the back of the shop leaving Lindy with a bemused look on her face. Lindy was embarrassed by this statement and didn't know what to say, but she realised that Margie was quite right—Brian was a good man, but she questioned whether she was ready for another relationship.

Caromar Cookies was growing and Caroline was struggling to keep up with supply to other businesses. It was obvious that they needed a more efficient way of distributing their cookies. Caroline thought it was time they had a van to do this, and she knew just whom she would like to employ.

At their next monthly meeting, which doubled as dinner with a few glasses of wine included, Caroline broached the subject of expanding the business and employing Brian to look after distributing their cookies to the other businesses that had enquired.

Margie pointed out that they didn't have a van, and it would be an expensive item to buy outright. Caroline hadn't mentioned that she had, through the Courts, forced Owen to hand over the money he stole from her when he had illegally sold Betty. It was likely that he would be charged with fraud as he had forged her signature and sold the car without her permission. The case was still pending for the return of her inheritance and it could be some months before that was settled. In the meantime Owen was in a mental health facility receiving treatment for his unstable personality. The police had told Caroline that he had demanded over and over again on admission to the facility that his papers be marked that his wife was not to come and harass him. Caroline told the police constable that there wasn't much chance of that happening. He was out of her life and she hoped he stayed there.

Caroline suggested that they lease a van until they got this arm of the business up and running. The other three girls were stunned by her courage dealing with Owen, but once again Caroline had shown them how much she had grown in strength since that first batch of cookies had put coins in the red kettle.

It was decided that Caroline should ask Brian if he was interested in driving the van, as she was the one who had to organise the baking and distribution of the cookies. He was delighted and accepted the position with just one question. "But what am I going to be driving?"

"Well, that will depend on what you think is the best vehicle for the job. You and I will go shopping, but there is just one stipulation and that is the vehicle must be blue." He looked at her quizzically but decided not to ask why. He reasoned that if Caroline wanted him to know why he should be driving a blue van then at some point she would tell him.

They wrote a sign on the van, "Caromar Cookies – go well with a cuppa" and the logo was a red kettle pouring liquid into a cup. Only Margie and Caroline understood the significance of this logo, and the colour of the van, but they were not about to tell anyone.

Brian was happy working with Caroline but was even happier that he got to see Lindy quite a lot throughout the week. Their fifteen-minute coffee breaks extended into a dinner invitation, which Lindy nervously agreed to. She liked Brian a lot, and they had a shared interest in art. Although neither thought they would ever be a celebrated artist, this was not the purpose of the painting classes.

Lindy had met other single men and women, and many of them had lost their partners to cancer. They understood what a terrible journey it could be and were very supportive of each other. After art class it seemed to be a natural thing for them to go somewhere for coffee, a meal, or drinks, and it was a great social outlet for those who wanted to join in. Brian and Lindy enjoyed the company of others but were just as happy with each other.

Chapter 28

As the art classes progressed, it was apparent that Lindy had a real talent that had been neglected since high school and turned out some very good work. Brian encouraged her to exhibit a few of her paintings in the coffee shop and after a lot of badgering she eventually gave in. She chose two small works, had them framed, and they looked lovely on the wall. She carefully printed up a small card with a modest price and was delighted when she came in a few days later and the paintings had been sold.

She questioned the girls about the buyer of her work, but they said they had never seen the lady before, but she wanted to know if Lindy had any other work that she could have a look at. The mystery buyer had said that she would come back in on Friday morning to meet Lindy and talk to her about a possible exhibition. Lindy just stood there with a stunned look on her face. The girls just laughed, as Lindy had never been stuck for words.

She was so excited that she rang Brian straight away, and he was delighted for her. They went out that night for a celebratory glass of champagne, which actually turned into a meal and a bottle of champagne; Lindy was so happy, and she felt she was building a new life. She still wasn't sure about her relationship with Brian, but she did enjoy his company. Their conversation never hit a silent patch, and she really looked forward to the next time she would see him. For now, she would just go with that and see where it led. He wasn't pressuring her, but she was starting to feel that he would like her to be a permanent part of his life, especially when he started talking about how maybe they could go on holidays together.

For Lindy, that would mean taking their relationship to another level. She was starting to enjoy having her hand held, a man's arm about her shoulders as she crossed the road and just the feel of someone physically close to her. She realised just how much she had missed the touch of another human being since her beloved husband had died.

On Friday morning, a nicely dressed woman came into the shop and asked if she could see Lindy. She handed over a card with her name, Lucinda Mannis, and her business name, "Galleries Lucinda," with a city address and phone number. Lindy brought coffee for Lucinda and herself, and they sat at a corner table in the quieter area of the shop.

Lucinda explained to Lindy that she spent quite a lot of time going around the area and sourcing out work of unknown artists for her gallery. She had found some amazing talent and over the years had launched the careers of some now well-known artists.

Her gallery was really a hobby as one of her previous husbands had left her quite well off, and so she had created a business where she could showcase undiscovered talent. She asked Lindy if she had any more work she could see and was reassured that there were quite a few canvasses completed but not framed. The two women made arrangements for Lucinda to stay in town that night, and Lindy would pick her up the next morning from her accommodation and drive her to her home. They would have lunch together while Lucinda looked over Lindy's work. As soon as Lucinda left the coffee shop, Lindy rang Brian with the wonderful news, and he couldn't have been happier for her.

"Celebration tonight?" he asked, but Lindy said she was so excited she wouldn't be able to eat but suggested they meet up the next night after Lucinda had seen her work and she could fill him in on all the news, and hopefully it would be good news. Brian finished the call by telling Lindy she was amazing and he was so glad Lucinda had come into her life. She was smiling when she put down the phone and realised how much Brian was coming to mean to her.

The next morning, Lindy took Lucinda to her home and shyly showed her the work she had created over the last year. She left Lucinda to have a look at the work as she quietly went out to make them each a coffee, served of course with a Caromar cookie.

Lucinda sat down to have her coffee and she had a big smile on her face.

"You have real talent, Lindy. It is a bit raw, but it is there".

Lindy was delighted and was even more so when Lucinda suggested that there were ten paintings that she particularly liked and she wanted to exhibit them in a mixed group of other artists she had found on this trip. She explained to Lindy that there was not enough for her to have a solo exhibition (which Lindy had never even thought possible a week ago), but with a mix of artists it would give depth and bring in more buyers.

"What do you think?" she asked Lindy. "Would you be prepared to give it a go?" Lindy just sat there stunned when Lucinda mentioned the type of prices that people would probably pay for her work, even though she was an unknown, because there was a quality that was evident although some of her technique still needed maturity.

Lindy jumped up from the table and flung her arms around the surprised Lucinda, saying, "Yes, yes, and yes. What do I need to do next?" Over lunch, arrangements were made for the framing, packing, and transport of the work to the gallery in the city. Lindy had hardly touched her lunch when it was time for Lucinda to go back to her hotel and pick up her car for the journey home.

She assured Lindy that she had had a very successful trip and was looking forward to putting the exhibition together. It was to be held in three months, and she would regularly be in touch with Lindy as the opening was going to be a black tie affair. *What am I going to wear?*

As soon as she could she rang Brian and told him the good news. She said that dinner out would be a waste of time and money as she was so excited she doubted she could eat anything. She suggested that he bring a bottle of champagne to her place, and she would "throw something together," which in Lindy's case was likely to be very well put together, using recipes that flowed from her brain to her hands, without any apparent effort.

Brian arrived at seven as arranged with a bottle of very expensive champagne in his hands. When just inside the door he gave Lindy a light hug and a kiss on the cheek and said, "Congratulations. You will be a success, and I wish you every bit of luck possible." Lindy was taken aback as she hadn't really processed that this could be the start of a whole new life for her, doing something she loved. However, she was wise enough to know that any future success depended largely on how the public perceived her paintings.

She knew that Lucinda was not taking all that much of a gamble, although she had been generous enough to include Lindy in a mixed exhibition, as profits mattered very little to her. As she had told Lindy, the gallery was her hobby, and she lived off her various investments left to her by a generous, now-departed husband. Nevertheless, Lindy was grateful for the chance to show her work, and in the city, which was even better.

Brian opened the champagne and when their glasses were full, they toasted the possibility of Lindy being the next newly discovered artist and the world that would open up for her. His toast, however, was tinged with sadness that she may move away from the town and their budding relationship would wither and die. He was starting to have feelings for Lindy that he never thought he would have for a woman again.

--oOo--

Chapter 29

Amanda was single and pregnant with a child conceived with her married lover. He would never know about his child if that were at all possible. Amanda wanted the child for herself, not for her lover. It was doubtful that Damien would try to find her, even though he had protested his undying love. No doubt he had promised to honour and obey his pregnant wife too.

Her lover was overseas on a company trip when Amanda handed in her notice, to take effect immediately. The human resources manager was shocked, but Amanda demeanour showed that no questions would be answered. Amanda knew that it would have a financial impact on her severance cheque, but that was the least of her concerns. She just needed to be absent when Damien returned. No one in the company thought to email the information to Damien while he was away, because the majority of her work colleagues were unaware that Amanda and Damien were "an item." It would just be a case of trying to replace Amanda before he returned so that his work could continue without a wrinkle in the spreadsheet.

Amanda just closed up her apartment in the city, rang some removalists who packed everything for her, and her belongings were put in storage until she could give them a forwarding address. Amanda remembered a country town where she and Damien had spent one of their illicit weekends, visiting wineries, having endless cups of coffee, and making love every chance they got.

When she arrived in the town she felt as though she had come home. She took a drive around the streets and pulled up in front of a real estate office. Within minutes she was enquiring for somewhere to rent and found a lovely cottage with a neat garden, just out of town, and within her now-limited budget. It was just a matter of arranging for her furniture to come from the city and she would have a home where she could rest until her baby was born.

The cottage was old, but it was in excellent condition and just needed a good clean, something that Amanda was not averse to doing. Her nesting instincts were in full swing as she went into the town hardware store and stocked up on all that she would need to make her new abode her own. After that she needed to start getting the nursery ready for her baby.

Next she made an appointment to see the obstetrician at the local hospital to be booked in for the birth of her child. She was declared hale and hearty, and everything was going perfectly. When it came to putting down the father's name, Amanda chose "Not Applicable," which caused the receptionist's eyebrows to raise just a fraction. "We are not specifying then, are we?" asked the receptionist.

Amanda looked her right in the eye and said, "No, we are not. He is just the sperm donor." The receptionist wasn't quite sure how to put this in the section of the computer requesting "Name of Father" so she just wrote "Unknown.". That would be gossip enough at the pub that night. A new blow-in, she would tell her friends, pregnant and didn't know who the father was. Gossip time! She must also mention that this chick was not young—like, she would be probably as old as thirty! She would be watching what happened with this one.

Amanda's pregnancy was trouble free and in the week that her due date fell, she went into labour. She drove herself the short distance to the hospital and only a few hours later gave birth to her healthy little girl. It was love at first sight for Amanda and as she held her darling girl to her breast she vowed to always be there for her and give her the best life she possibly could. After a day and a night in hospital, Amanda and Jamie went home to their little cottage and the newly decorated nursery.

Amanda was sad that her mother had not been in contact. They had had quite a row when Rebecca was informed she was going to be a grandma. Her retort was, "You fool. Don't you know how hard it is going to be for you to bring up a child by yourself?"

Amanda had just calmly answered, "Well you did it, Mum and I don't see why I can't." The phone being slammed down by Rebecca ended that conversation. Amanda had deliberately become pregnant but not as a result of a drunken night with a Spanish tour operator. Her mother's words had wounded her deeply because she wasn't a fool and had been genuinely looking forward to having her darling daughter. The similarity then struck her that Jaimie was as unlikely to see her father as Amanda had been.

Jamie was a happy, peaceful baby, feeding when she should and sleeping soundly. Amanda couldn't resist peeking at her while she slept and kept Jamie out of her cot for as long as possible while she cuddled her and walked around with her in a sling thing while she prepared meals.

When Jamie was six months old, Amanda was running out of savings and needed to get a job so hooked her computer up to the Internet. While Jamie was sleeping she searched out courses she could do online with a view to employment, the emphasis being on helping other young women in the same position as her—single mothers. On her visits to town she had seen a few young mums with bubs in prams but had been hesitant to strike up any friendships. She wasn't ready yet for awkward questions about a "husband."

Occasionally she had stopped at the Coffee Pot for a latte on one of her long walks around town. She had met Caroline, the maker of cookies for the coffee shop, on several occasions and had always been friendly to her. Caroline always enquired about Jamie, how she was doing, how much weight she had put on, etc., but had never asked about Jamie's father, for which Amanda was grateful. She still wasn't sure what she wanted to answer to that question.

There was very little time to chat because Caroline and the owner, whom Amanda hadn't seen yet, were trying to build up the business with good service, great coffee, and some very tasty snacks. There were plenty of good restaurants in town, but this coffee shop was trying to find its niche in the market. Their mission was to provide tasty cookies or snacks, not available anywhere else in the town, which were great with a coffee.

During her Government Department searches Amanda came across a funded scheme that had been formed to get training for single mothers so they could return to the workforce, either part time or full time. She had been given the contact name of Jennifer Simmons and arranged to meet her and discuss what was available.

Afterwards, it was apparent that there was work out there for someone with Amanda's corporate background and very little transitional training would be required. Amanda's was hopeful she could get a part-time marketing job in the local area. Jennifer provided her with the relevant paperwork and let her know where to lodge it but advised her to do it sooner rather than later because the retraining courses were filling up fast. Even though Amanda would probably not need much retraining, it was more a case of ticking the boxes on a government form that the course had been completed and thus provide eligibility to access a huge database and search for work.

Jennifer's workload was enormous, but she enjoyed the challenges that the job brought, not to mention the good salary. As her "girls" went through and found jobs, it certainly gave her a sense of accomplishment and one of her favourite students was Amanda Watkins. She was intelligent, hard working, gave 100% all of the time, and Jennifer knew she would be a success at whatever she took on.

Another of her favourites was Lindy, who she had placed with Margie at the Coffee Pot, and she had helped make that business a success with her hard work, pleasant manner, and knowledge of running a small business. Jennifer liked following up on how her girls were going in their new careers.

Within a short time Amanda had been offered a sales rep job with a printing company, which was supposed to be part time, according to the advertisement, but it wasn't working out that way at all. Fortunately, some of the work could be done at home, but it also required quite a lot of travelling on other days. She had her daughter to look after and didn't want to be away from her for very long at all. She had tried having a live-in babysitter but after a few occasions of finding the nubile young lady in bed with the latest boyfriend when she should have been looking after Jamie, that arrangement was terminated.

She next tried a local mother who was allowed, under Council regulations, to mind two children in her home. Amanda arrived early one afternoon at the baby-sitter's home and found eight children being cared for. This was not what she had signed up for, and so she took Jamie home until she could work out what to do. There was no point asking her mother for help as that door had firmly been shut.

The next day Amanda went to the coffee shop and asked one of the part-time girls if she could put a card on their notice board to advertise for a baby-sitter, as she knew she would need help with Jamie but wanted someone local. Margie saw the card and wondered if this was the same Amanda Watkins that had lived with her and her ex-husband all those years ago. She phoned the number on the card and announced who she was. She was nearly deafened by the scream on the other end of the phone: "Margie, oh my God is it really you? I haven't heard from you in so long? Where are you? Can we meet up?" They arranged to meet that afternoon and talked non-stop for hours.

Amanda told Margie how her mother had moved them from place to place following a man or a job and over the years they had changed their addresses so many times, it wasn't surprising that they had lost contact. Rebecca was not pleased that Amanda had chosen to go down the path of single parenthood as she knew how hard it had been for her, even with Margie and Ron's help, but it was Amanda's choice to bring her daughter up by herself.

The contact between Amanda and her mother was not improving with any great speed and was sporadic at best. It was certainly not very satisfying on either side. Rebecca had only seen photos of her granddaughter, and this upset Amanda, but she couldn't make her mother do what she didn't want to. Rebecca would rather go off on an unplanned Girls Weekend than have to schedule in time to see her Jamie. Part of her absence was because Rebecca didn't want to be seen out and about with her granddaughter as she felt it aged her in other people's eyes. She very much wanted to be a walking advertisement for the Fountain of Youth and every spare cent was spent on the Beautification of Rebecca.

Margie then offered to look after Jamie, as she was already minding Gavin in her home. He would be at school the next year but in the meantime would be a great help to Gamma, as he called Margie, and the two children could be company for each other.

Amanda was thrilled, as she knew how well Margie had looked after her when she had been little and had every confidence that her daughter would be cared for in the same way.

Later that day Margie took Amanda to her home and introduced her to Caroline, who was working away in the kitchen making the next day's cookies. Margie was amazed when the girls threw their arms around each other. "How do you know each other?" she asked, and the girls told her how they had already been chatting, unaware that Margie had been a big influence in Amanda's young life. They started talking away like old friends, and their two children played together quite happily while coffee and cookies were served. By the end of the afternoon, Margie had arranged for Gavin and Jamie to be in her care and she couldn't have been happier. She was helping out two women in her life that had become very dear to her—one when she was a child and the other when she was an adult. Life couldn't be better.

Chapter 30

Amanda had negotiated shorter hours with the printing company, but the travelling sometimes meant that she would be late getting to Margie's place for Jamie. Margie solved this problem by assuring Amanda that she would feed and bathe Jamie so she would be ready to go home when her mother came to collect her. Amanda was delighted, and Margie's heart was full that she could help out these two young women who held a very special place in her heart.

Margie minded Gavin until he went to school and then looked after him until Caroline could pick him up in the afternoon. Amanda was becoming tired of the travelling and was not happy that she didn't see Jamie as much as she would like. She knew there would be special days at school that she would want to attend and didn't think the printing company would be all that flexible for too long. She felt she needed a change and had been studying up on the latest marketing trends while Jamie slept each night. Amanda had never been a party girl and therefore didn't miss the city's buzz. She just wanted to earn a good living, doing something she loved, and being around for her darling daughter.

She asked Margie if she could speak with her, Caroline, and Lindy, as she had a proposal she would like them to consider. They decided that they would go out to dinner and chose a quiet restaurant nearby where they could talk without much background noise. Once they were all settled and had drinks in their hands, Margie asked, "So, what is this all about, Amanda?"

She had made up a presentation in book form for each of them, and in it she detailed her proposal. She told them that she wanted to leave the printing company to have more to do with Jamie's life when she started school and was tired of the travelling. She knew there would be sports days and other important occasions, and she wanted to be available to attend. She remembered that when she was young, her mother was working so hard to keep them afloat that she was never able to go and only got the information second hand from Amanda some time after the event. Amanda didn't want that for Jamie, so it was time to change employment.

The girls ordered their meal and while they were waiting Amanda suggested that she would do their marketing for them and outlined her plan as they followed her booklet through. She would be her own company and would charge them for whatever work she completed. She reassured them that she would be totally transparent with what work she did and would give them an updated report every month.

Caroline and Lindy wanted the business to expand. On one hand, Margie did too but was aware that she was getting older and would really like some time to just smell the roses. She would not have Gavin and Jamie to take care of forever and would have a lot of time on her hands, but she thought she would rather semi-retire and work on her Wish List of Things to Do before I Turn 100.

Margie had always fancied going on a cruise to an exotic location, doing a shopping trip to Paris, even though she knew she would be horrified at the prices, but she didn't want to just rust away either. While Amanda had been speaking, Margie had realised that more than anything she would like to contact her friend, Rebecca, Amanda's mother. They'd had a great friendship, but circumstances for them both meant it had been almost twenty years since they had been in touch and she wanted to remedy that. In the back of her mind she also realised that it could help bring Amanda and her mother closer together if she was in the general vicinity seeing Margie.

Margie realised that to step back from the business would mean a loss of control, to a certain extent, but the three women were more than capable of running each part of it autonomously: Caroline with new recipes and production, Lindy with the retail side, and Amanda to do the promotion of Caromar Cookies. The girls noticed that Margie was quiet and asked, almost as one voice, "Are you okay with this Margie? We haven't trodden on your toes, have we?"

"I couldn't be happier that you three girls will be working together to build the business that was started to keep me fed and clothed when Ron and I got divorced."

The other three women thought it was a great idea, but to do this they would need to have a greater manufacturing capacity or they wouldn't be able to keep up supply. They suggested that Amanda put this idea on the back burner, just for a while, until they got a factory set up. This was really scary for them because none of them even anticipated that Caromar Cookies would be so popular and successful. They realised that Margie's kitchen was often at the bursting point with cookies, wrapping paper, jars, price tags, and promotional material and they had reached the time when they would either stay as they were or expand. Fortunately, they were all on the same wavelength and expansion was what they all wanted. Or was it?

Lindy dropped a bombshell. "I was actually going to ask for three months leave," she announced to the astonished women in front of her. As one voice they said, "Why?" Lindy told them about Lucinda and her offer to Lindy to see if she had any talent as a professional artist, but she needed time to prepare for the proposed exhibition. There was silence for just a moment, and then there were three women hugging her and wishing her well.

Margie was a bit stunned and knew she would miss her capable manager but was also aware that Lindy needed to try this venture and see how she went. The girls told Lindy that they would cover for her for the three months and any plans would be put on hold until she tested the waters of becoming a professional artist.

Chapter 31

I t was a gruelling three months for Lindy as she prepared her work for framing, transport, and hanging in the very classy Galleries Lucinda. On one visit to the gallery to check where her work would be hung, she was daunted when she saw some of the other paintings already on the walls.

Lucinda quietly came up to her and said, "Don't be concerned, Lindy. Your work is equally good but is different, so please don't compare." Lucinda went on to say that she had hung in her office the two paintings she had purchased from the coffee shop and many people had commented on how lovely they were. This cheered Lindy up a bit, and she went home with a spring in her step, prepared to tackle the job of framing before arranging transport to the city.

Caroline came and asked Lindy how the exhibition was progressing and found her friend knee deep in bubble wrap, tape, and packing materials. Brian was helping too, but he didn't look very happy about this whole venture. When Lindy left the room to go and make some coffee, Caroline could sense that Brian wasn't his usual cheery self.

"What's up, Brian?" Caroline asked. "Aren't you happy about this?"

"Yes of course I am happy for Lindy, but I just hope she isn't too disappointed if she doesn't sell anything."

"Well, we will just have to go to the opening of the exhibition, all dressed up in our glad rags, and give her all the support she deserves. After that it is up to the public."

"I hope you're right," Brian replied just as Lindy came into the room.

"Right about what?" Lindy asked as she put the coffee cups and cookies onto the table.

"Oh we were just hoping that the exhibition is a success for you. It might be the start of a new career, and it may take you right out of our orbit."

Lindy looked thoughtful when she replied, "Nothing is going to remove me from your orbit, as you put it. I love you girls like sisters, and well, Brian is a love on a completely different level."

Brian blushed under Caroline's scrutiny when she uttered, "Well, what a dark horse you are, Lindy. And here am I thinking you are just friends. Good for both of you, and I can't wait to tell everyone else. I can, can't I? It is not a secret?"

Lindy and Brian hugged each other and laughingly drew Caroline in with them. "Not anymore," said Brian.

To get the artwork to the city would require transport, so it was mutually decided that the Caromar Cookies van would be just the thing. Caroline mentioned that it would also be advertising on four wheels, and maybe someone in the city would see it and again they could grow the business.

"But we are not doing any expanding until you come back from the big smoke and we know what your decision is about your future," Caroline confirmed.

"It is your life, Lindy, and you only get one shot at it, so do what makes your heart happy. You know we all wish you every happiness whatever you choose to do, and we will back you all the way."

The exhibition was a resounding success and even on the first night there were red dots on several of Lindy's paintings, and Brian was so proud of her that it seemed as though his chest would break through the pearl buttons on his new shirt. Lucinda was thrilled at the way Lindy's paintings were selling and reassured her they would stay on the walls for eight weeks at least. In the meantime if she had a mind to paint any more, they could be put up as well.

Lindy was exhausted at the end of the night, and though she was pleased with the exhibition, she realised that it wasn't really her thing to stand around with a champagne glass in her hand and chat to people who seemed a bit superficial to her way of thinking. She was used to being with real people and that was when she decided professional artist was not on her wish list. She had missed the daily contact with her regular customers, the hustle and bustle of the shop, and realised that while painting made her creative side come alive, it was a lonely pursuit. She had hardly any time to catch up with friends while she did extra paintings for the exhibit and had missed their company.

When they got back to the city hotel where they were staying, they all gathered in Lindy's room to celebrate her success. They had taken turns going back to the hotel to look after Gavin and Jamie when it was their bedtime. Scott had come to the exhibition but had to go on to a company dinner. He was really pleased for his mother and was introduced to Brian. He was happy his mother had a new man in her life to really care for Lindy.

Ruby had sent an exotic gown from somewhere in the Far East for Lindy to wear at the exhibition and she looked wonderful in it. There would be photos on Facebook for Ruby to see how her choice of outfit had been so successful, although the girl didn't actually own a dress of her own. That would have been a bit superfluous to requirements when your main mission in life was saving animals in remote parts of the world.

When they were all seated in the hotel suite, Lindy made an announcement, and it caught everyone by surprise.

"I have something I would like to say," she started out. "Firstly, thank you all for your love, support, and being here with me tonight. I cannot tell you how much it means to have friends like you who are always there for me. I have made a decision."

There was a collective holding of breaths as they all thought Lindy would be leaving their small town and going to be a professional artist in the city, and they weren't looking forward to that announcement at all.

"I have decided that I want to resume my job at the coffee shop."
A loud cheer went up from all in the room. Once the hubbub had died
down she went on to say, "But I am going to work at the local drop-in
zone for troubled teens and see if I can help them deal with their
feelings through art."

Again, a loud cheer, but Lindy wasn't finished yet. "I also would
like to say that I couldn't possibly move to the city and leave behind
the most wonderful friends that anyone could wish to have. Also,
Brian and I are getting married." It was a moment or two until the
last statement registered with everyone and the noise of cheering and
handclapping was deafening. "You are all invited to the wedding,
because it wouldn't be the same without you."

Margie toasted Lindy and Brian's future and asked, "Can we take
the expansion plans off the back burner now?"

Lindy raised her glass and replied, "You sure can, Margie. I am
home to stay."

They were all delighted with the outcome of the evening and
especially that Lindy had found her niche with art and a man who
would stand by her no matter what life threw at them. And life was
about to throw Ruby at them.

She was not happy when she heard about her mother's engagement,
but when she returned home Lindy was going to make sure that Ruby
was made to understand that this didn't mean any disrespect to John,
but that she had been lonely and meeting Brian had been the start of a
new life for them. Ruby would always be difficult, but Lindy had come
to accept that was just the way her daughter was made.

--o0o--

Chapter 32

Margie realised that it had been at least ten years since she had been on holiday and was badly in need of one right now. Looking back she realised how much had happened in the last decade and just the thought made her feel tired.

She and Ron had separated and then divorced, she had bought the coffee shop and built the business up with Caroline, minded her two favourite children in the world, and caught up again with an old friend, Rebecca. The business was growing and would provide a good living for them all. Caroline and Amanda each had children, they had put deposits on homes for themselves, and now that Gavin and Jamie were at school she had a lot of spare time on her hands. Life was good, but Margie wanted to do something different with whatever years she had left.

She wasn't interested in craft very much and apart from attending the occasional charity fundraiser she had a lot of time on her hands. She didn't relish the thought of growing old and rusting out instead of wearing out. She needed a project, and travel seemed to be a good idea. It would broaden the mind, or so the travel agents said, but Margie just hoped it didn't broaden her hips with all the food available. She had seen coloured illustrations in the brochures, and it was enough to make your mouth water.

She had recently been in to a travel agent to check out what was available for a single traveller and with a bit of persuasion had decided to go on a cruise, especially geared towards those who were emotionally unattached. Margie certainly qualified on those grounds so paid her deposit and with a brochure in her hand left the travel agent to have a really strong coffee. She couldn't believe that she had actually booked to go on a singles cruise!

Margie had convinced herself that she wasn't looking for a man to be added to her already busy life, but when she went home at night and closed the door, the loneliness came in with her. Women who frequented the coffee shop often regaled her with hilarious tales of online dating and their successes and spectacular failures, and this had made Margie think that maybe trying to find a partner really wasn't worth the bother. She was of the opinion that no male would be as amenable as her dearly departed Prince, although she couldn't imagine a human male taking up as much room on her lap.

With a glass of wine in her hand after dinner, Margie sat down and opened the coloured brochure that promised so much more than what she thought she was looking for. There was a cabaret every night, a masked ball, captain's dinner, fitness sessions, painting, crafts, and the descriptions of the food available made her mouth water. However, she was still worried about doing this cruise alone.

She worried about almost every aspect of it. Would she take the right clothes, would she be able to sleep in a different and probably smaller space from what she was used to? Who would she be sitting with at the table? However, she kept all these fears to herself as she was conscious that it would sound ridiculous to most of the women she met who seemed to be so confident and getting on with life at a speed that terrified Margie. It was Fred this week, then Barry the next, followed by George, who was an absolute dud in bed. Too much information for Margie to absorb!

Margie finally took Caroline into her confidence and told her that she had signed up for a singles cruise. The look on Caroline's face was surprise, then pure joy. Caroline threw her arms around Margie's neck and gave her a huge hug. "Oh Margie, that is so adventurous. I am excited that you are having a holiday after all the hard work you have put into this place for all these years." She held Margie at arm's length and declared, "Well, I think a bit of retail therapy is in order, don't you?"

As the cruise was scheduled to depart in eight weeks, Caroline and Margie made a plan to get away early one Saturday and go to the nearest shopping village to outfit Margie with clothes that were suitable for a cruising lady. With a sense of excitement Caroline steered Margie towards the section of resort wear and laughed out aloud at the look of amazement on her friend's face when she turned over the first price tag. "Don't look at the price," Caroline gently admonished her. "Just check out the design and the colours."

Margie replied, "It's alright for you young things, but I don't want to look like mutton dressed up as lamb." Caroline just shook her head and took Margie over to a different rack of clothes that she thought would be more to her friend's liking.

Two hours passed with Caroline going backwards and forwards to the racks and bringing to the dressing room a different size or colour until Margie was happy with what she had chosen. She didn't dare add up the price tags, and Margie got back into her own clothes, scooped the outfits off the chair in the dressing room, and bravely approached the cash desk with her credit card in the other hand. The total wasn't nearly as horrific as she had expected, and with her tissue-wrapped resort wear safely in their bags, she and Caroline started off to find a well-earned coffee.

After only a few minutes, Margie made the statement, "I don't feel like coffee. This holiday is the start of something I have never done in my life and I want to celebrate with champagne." Caroline was happy to go along with that, and together they found a lovely wine bar and ordered a bottle of the best champagne they could afford. Not being used to alcohol, they didn't need more than a glass or two before they were both giggling and anticipating scenarios when Margie would be wearing her resort wear.

When they got back to Margie's place they unpacked the bags and had a really good look at what had been purchased and a fashion parade followed, but not before they had rung Lindy and Amanda to come over and see what their shopping had achieved. The other two girls brought champagne and some snacks as they felt too that it was about time Margie had a good holiday. The four of them had a wonderful evening and a bit of a hangover the next day, but they were all sure that Margie would look great in what she had chosen.

There seemed to be an outfit for any occasion, and Margie had even been persuaded to buy some sexy lingerie, though she had protested strongly that she wouldn't need it because nobody would be seeing what was under her clothes. The girls all hoped that someone would get an eyeful, as it was a singles cruise, after all. Under the influence of alcohol, the question of "What about if you meet someone and want to go to bed with them?" emerged.

Margie just threw some cushions at the three of them and stated vehemently, "What I haven't had I won't miss."

By midnight the party was breaking up, and the girls went home, in taxis, to their respective addresses. The next morning their mobile phones were running hot checking with each other about what they thought about Margie's outfits and whether she would strike it lucky and meet someone on the cruise.

The girls talked Margie into having her decade-old hairstyle revamped, go for some beauty treatments, a pedicure, manicure, and a massage. Margie put up some token resistance, but she was secretly pleased that "her girls" were so happy for her and excited that she was at last doing something for herself, instead of doing things for everybody else.

The date of the cruise was getting closer, and Margie was becoming nervous. "What if I have done the wrong thing? I might get seasick. I might be homesick. I might hate seeing water all around me. I might not be asked to dance. I might have the wrong clothes. I might be lonely." Her girls brushed all of these protests off and reassured her that she would have a wonderful time, even though none of them had ever been on a cruise. They just knew that they all wanted Margie to have a fantastic time.

Margie left it until the last part of the day that she was required to pay the rest of the cruise money. She protested, she procrastinated, she put it off for as long as possible, and by the time there was only a half-hour left to get to the travel agent Caroline threatened to tie her up and drag her there if necessary. Margie was going on this cruise—no matter what!

The rest of the money was put on her credit card, and she emerged from the travel agent with a folder full of information for this singles cruise. Margie couldn't believe the amount of things that this holiday promised and all in glowing detail. As soon as she came in the door of the coffee shop, Caroline and Lindy came across to her with big smiles on their faces.

"You only have to pack your suitcase now," said Caroline.

Lindy added, "And don't leave out that sexy underwear either, because we will be doing a final inspection of your luggage, and it had better be in there." Margie just laughed and turned away from them, but she had a big smile on her face, and now that it was only five days away she was getting quite excited.

Chapter 33

It was the day of the cruise, and Margie didn't know whether the butterflies in her stomach were from excitement or fear. The girls made sure she had everything she needed in her luggage, and Caroline drove her to the airport for her flight to the city where she was due to board the ship at six that night. They got there in plenty of time and after Caroline had gotten the luggage out of the car, she gave Margie a big hug and wished her the best holiday ever. As Caroline drove off she could see Margie still standing outside the glass doors to the airport terminal, looking a little lost.

After checking her bag she wandered slowly to the lounge area to await the announcement of her flight. She started to read her book, but when she had read the same page three times, she decided she would put it away until she actually boarded the flight. She wasn't scared of flying but didn't like the take-off and landing very much and started to chew on her brand-new acrylic nails. When she realised what she was doing she put her hands in her pockets. It wouldn't do to start off a singles cruise with bitten-down nails that had cost her forty-five dollars applied only yesterday.

In the destination city, she got a taxi from the airport to the cruise terminal, and it wasn't long before the "all aboard" call went out to the passengers, most of whom were standing alone just looking around at who else might be on board. The passengers were a mixed group of ages and Margie was pleased that quite a large percentage was in the over-40 time of their life. Some might say they were in their 40s but Margie was more inclined to believe that what they really meant was that they were born in the 40s, which put a whole different spin on their actual age. Never mind, a little white lie now and again didn't hurt anyone, and if they wanted to drop a decade then that was their business.

The ship's representative at the top of the gangway checked Margie's ticket off his list, welcomed her aboard with a very cheery voice, told her she was going to have a marvellous time, that her cabin number was 12b, and gave her directions how to find it. It was obvious from the confusion in some of the corridors that finding the right cabin was challenging for certain passengers.

She was pleasantly surprised to see that she had a cabin with a balcony, although she realised that must have been mentioned in the brochure somewhere. All those coloured squares on a deck plan just totally confused her. When she'd booked, she was too worried about how she was going to cope on her own. There was a light tapping on the door and Margie called out, "Come in," and who should appear but Rebecca.

Margie just gaped at her in astonishment. "What are you doing here?" She asked her when she finally got her voice back after almost squashing Rebecca with a hug.

"I couldn't let you loose on the men by yourself," she replied. "The girls kept it a secret from you, because they wanted it to be a surprise." Margie just shook her head in wonder and gave her another hug.

"Oh Rebecca, it will be just like old times, and I have missed your friendship so much over the years. I hope we never lose contact again." Rebecca had tears in her eyes and a lump in her throat, being with her friend who had made such a difference in her life at a time when she most needed someone to be a friend. She too regretted the years that they had missed out on by not being in touch.

After unpacking, the girls decided to go upstairs and investigate what was available on the daily timetable. They were both determined to not miss a thing that was on option, whether it was a salsa class or a tour in port. They were so happy to be in each other's company again after such a long time apart and didn't stop talking until it was time to go back to the cabin and dress for dinner.

Margie went through her dresses until she found something she thought was suitable, but when Rebecca spied the rather ordinary outfit, which Margie had sneaked into her luggage from her previous life, as she now thought of it, Rebecca took hold of it and threw it back in the wardrobe. "You can't wear that old thing." She reached into the wardrobe and found a brightly coloured outfit that did wonderful things for Margie's colouring.

"But I will stand out" Margie wailed.

"That's the general idea," laughed Rebecca. "We are on a singles cruise remember, and we are not the only women here." After a bit more persuading, Margie put on the beautiful printed silk peacock-blue and magenta top with matching peacock-blue pants and she looked amazing. When her hair was done to Rebecca's satisfaction, and the appropriate jewellery decorating her neck and ears, Margie was allowed to look in the mirror. She couldn't believe what she saw, but was so glad Rebecca had taken the previous-life outfit and thrown it back in the wardrobe. Then it was Rebecca's turn, and Margie had no cause to criticise what her friend was wearing. The years had given her a style all her own, and she looked like a cross between a gypsy and an exotic Eastern princess.

They looked and felt absolutely wonderful and arm in arm set out to find the dining room. On arrival they were advised that drawing a number out of a hat and finding the corresponding number on a table plan arranged the seating. This meant that Margie and Rebecca probably wouldn't be sitting together, but that didn't matter to either of them as they wanted to meet new people, and this was a great way to do it. It also meant that they would probably be with different people each night for dinner.

When seated Margie found that there were five women and three men at her table and they all started asking each other's name and where they were from. This was a real icebreaker, and it wasn't long before the conversation flowed readily from one diner to another. The food was exceptionally good, and Margie was glad that the loose top she had on would cover any tummy bulge gained by the end of the meal. It occurred to her that if this was the standard and quantity of the meals, she had better watch how much she ate—but it was all so yummy and hard to resist dessert.

Throughout the meal the MC spoke on the microphone and told the diners what was on the program for that night and salsa lessons in the ballroom seemed to be the main attraction, judging by the rousing cheer when he mentioned this activity. As it was a singles cruise they had an interesting way of matching people up. There were two buckets with numbered tickets in them—pink for women and blue for men. The women slightly outnumbered the men so some tickets for women were blank, whereas all the males had a numbered ticket. Everyone who wanted to participate dipped in the bucket for a ticket and then had to set about finding their partner with the same number. Those ladies who had a blank ticket got to choose from the bucket first for the next dance. There was a lot of laughter trying to track down a partner in the allotted two minutes, and then it was on to learning the salsa.

Rebecca and Margie had a wonderful night, nicely topped up with some champagne, and wandered down the corridor to find cabin 12b. Their internal compasses were a little off the beam, probably courtesy of the bubbly, and they couldn't work out why their key wouldn't work in the door of cabin 21b. A few more giggles and they eventually found their room just down the corridor on the other side.

Before they went to bed they decided to have an early-morning swim, but somehow the late night and alcohol took its toll and it was nine before their morning actually started. They hastily dressed in casual clothes and headed for the dining room at a fast pace as breakfast finished at nine-thirty and they didn't want to miss out. This was not organised seating, and the girls found a table right next to a window where they could watch the ocean going by. To their absolute delight they spied some whales just off the port side and were amazed at how that amount of mammal managed to lift itself so far out of the water. They were joking with each other that if they kept eating as much as they had in the last twelve hours they would probably strongly represent that whale out there but doubted if they could lift themselves out of the swimming pool.

Breakfast over and done with, too late for a swim, they scanned the activities board for the day. Nothing really caught their fancy except a fashion parade that would be held that afternoon in the ballroom, followed by a floorshow spectacular after dinner. Their holiday was off to a wonderful start.

They both received emails from Caroline, Amanda, and Lindy to wish them well and asking Margie if she got a surprise. She reprimanded them for keeping Rebecca's plans secret, but she was delighted that they had even thought of it.

It would make her holiday just that bit better. She told them about the salsa lessons and her aching hips, the fashion parade that was going to be on that afternoon and even mentioned that she might, but only might, buy some clothes to add to her increasing wardrobe. She didn't tell them that Rebecca had gone through her clothes and discarded all those from her previous life as being entirely unsuitable for a warm-hearted, romantic, intelligent, and temporarily single lady.

They dressed for dinner again that night and were excited about which table they might be placed at and with whom. Margie was seated across from a very nice-looking gentleman about her own age. He had lovely thick grey hair, twinkling blue eyes, and was dressed very smartly. The conversation flowed around the table, and when dinner was over and the diners had dispersed to the cocktail bar, George came over and asked if Margie would like a drink. Rebecca was nowhere to be seen, so Margie thanked him and accepted his offer.

They took their drinks to a quieter corner of the bar, and he mentioned that he was planning to go to the floorshow spectacular later that evening. Margie confirmed that she and Rebecca were planning to be there too, and George asked if they would both like to share a table with him. She was very attracted to him and his lovely way of speaking. He seemed to be a real gentleman, but Margie had heard of disappointments in budding romances before with many a wolf in sheep's clothing.

The floorshow was fantastic, but Margie still hadn't sighted Rebecca after dinner. She wasn't concerned because they had agreed they would do their own thing and not be stuck at the hip. Rebecca was quite capable of looking after herself and was usually careful with how much alcohol she drank. Margie and George sat together throughout the show and when it came time to leave, he asked if he could escort her to her cabin. Margie hesitated and George quickly said, "Only to the door, Margie, that's all." She smiled at him and told him the cabin number. They strolled down the corridor and George smiled at Margie and thanked her for her wonderful company and hoped to see her tomorrow. Margie was relieved that he wasn't being pushy because she wasn't too sure about how she would handle that, but she didn't need to worry.

Rebecca turned up about an hour later and drifted in the door with a huge smile on her face. "I have just met the most fabulous man," she purred. "He is a bit younger than me, but oh so sexy." She went on about him for another thirty minutes without seeming to take a breath and all Margie could do was laugh. When she had regaled Margie with all the details of her night, she asked, "So, what did you do? I didn't see you after dinner." Rebecca's mouth dropped open when Margie told her about George, the cocktail bar, and the floorshow. "Gee, girl, you haven't wasted any time, have you?" she laughed.

"Well, neither have you," Margie fired back with a smile on her face.

Chapter 34

It was the early hours of the morning before they both settled down to go to sleep and decided that an early morning swim probably wasn't on their agenda for tomorrow but maybe the next day. With late nights and late mornings, Margie doubted they would ever even see the pool in daylight.

At breakfast, George appeared looking very handsome and freshly showered. He waved at Margie and Rebecca, but he was just leaving the dining room, and Margie was a bit disappointed he didn't come over and say hello.

They filled in their day with some fitness activities; supposedly to work off last night's dinner, but with what they had consumed it would have required a ten-kilometre run around the ship. Their kilojoule intake was fast outstripping their kilojoule output and increasing kilos would no doubt be the result. They agreed they would worry about that when they got home. It was such a joy to have meals already prepared and served to you by some of the cutest waiters they had seen.

When they were queuing up for dinner they noticed a tired and rather dishevelled group of people coming on board, and George was amongst them. He certainly didn't look as suave as he had that morning, but Margie was relieved to know he hadn't been on the ship all day and avoiding her.

An hour later, George reappeared in the dining room and looked much better. He waved to Margie and sat down at his table, and as soon as dinner was finished he came over and told her about his day. The small boat they had gone ashore on had had engine trouble and that was why they were late getting back. One of the passengers had wandered off and it was some time before they located her; she was lucky that the boat hadn't left on time for the ship or she would have been stranded with all her souvenirs.

Rebecca had managed to track down her toy-boy, as they now referred to him, and she was off to the disco she informed Margie, "See you later." She smiled and disappeared around the corner arm in arm with Alexander. Margie was very dubious that she would actually see Rebecca later, as something in her smile told her she may not come back to the cabin at all. *Good for her, it is a long time since she has been so happy.*

The next day was the halfway point of the cruise so there were lots of activities on the deck and people had to be chosen as the Halfway King and Halfway Queen. This title came with suitably ridiculous dressing up so they looked as though they had been dredged from the deep blue sea. Margie was mortified when she was chosen to wear a long blond wig, which looked like it had seen better days, and a skirt type thing that was supposed to be a mermaid's tail. She was covered in shell necklets and shell anklets and could hardly stop laughing when she saw what she looked like in the window's reflection. The Halfway King didn't look much better than she did, but at least he didn't have to wear itchy shells around his neck and ankles.

They had a wonderful time and really played up to their parts. They were brought food on platters piled high with fruit and prawns. Their drinks arrived in coconut shells that had been hulled out, but the liquid in it looked like pineapple juice and smelt like rocket fuel. Goodness only knows what had gone into it but when Margie, hampered by her mermaid's tail, went to stand up, she was more than a little unsteady on her feet. It certainly didn't help the situation that she had been sitting in the sun for a few hours. There was lots of laughter and people being thrown in the pool, but all Margie wanted to do was put her head down on the pillow and stop the world spinning around.

George wasn't far away and noticed that she didn't look all that well so he came over and asked if she was okay. Margie shook her head, which wasn't really a good idea, so George took her arm and guided her towards her cabin. She said she would get out of the ridiculous costume and have a rest for a while to stop the world going around. When she was settled in the cabin George asked if he could ring her in a few hours to see how she was feeling. Margie mumbled her mobile number and hoped that it made sense to him. There was no sign of Rebecca, but Margie assumed that she would be with her new love, somewhere on the ship.

Her phone rang about six and it was George checking if she was okay and would she be going up to dinner. The thought of eating dinner made her feel quite ill but she agreed to meet him out on the deck at about eight so she could get some fresh air and perhaps some fruit juice but not the one with the rocket fuel in it. George just laughed at her description of the drink and said he looked forward to seeing her later.

Margie showered and dressed in casual clothes, threw a jacket around her shoulders, and went up on deck to meet George. She was more than pleasantly surprised when he showed her to a table he had asked the waiter to organise, and on it was some beautifully presented fruit, crackers, and cheese. "I thought you might be a bit hungry by now," he said and Margie thanked him for his thoughtfulness. He was certainly a nice man and she was very taken with him but quite unsure if this was just a shipboard romance or something more.

He had told Margie that he was a widower with two grown-up daughters who lived interstate so he didn't see much of them and his three grandchildren. She told him that she hadn't been fortunate enough to have any children, and he listened quietly while she told him how it had been the reason that she and Ron had broken up. She told him about Rebecca and how she had known her for such a long time, but they hadn't seen each other for years until recently. She and Amanda had been a big part of her life for eleven years when she had been married to Ron, but time and moving for jobs and romances had taken Rebecca away from her.

She was so grateful that the girls had organised this holiday, even though she hadn't seen much of Rebecca since Alexander had come on the scene. Margie suspected that Rebecca and Alexander were the epitome of a shipboard romance, but who cared? They seemed happy in each other's company for the time being.

During the time they were sitting at the table outside on the deck, the night breeze had come up, and George lightly placed Margie's jacket around her shoulders and gave her a kiss on the top of her head but left his hands where they were. Margie tilted her head back and George gave her a soft kiss on her forehead, her nose, and then her mouth.

Margie was in no doubt that she liked George a lot but wasn't sure where she wanted this to go, if anywhere at all. She was so out of practise and hadn't really had any men in her life since she divorced Ron. She had been working too hard to find time for a male, except her cat Prince, and the girls and their children took up most of her spare time. It was only when George put his arms around her that she realised how much she had been missing.

It was getting towards midnight when he suggested they go back inside. The ballroom was emptying after the second show for the night, and Margie spied Rebecca arm in arm with Alexander and heading in completely the opposite direction to cabin 12b.

George put his arm through Margie's and guided her towards the cocktail bar and enquired if she was sufficiently recovered to have a glass of rather delicious champagne. They clinked glasses and wished each other a great day tomorrow. He asked her if she would like another glass of champagne, but instead of sitting in the cocktail bar, would she prefer to have it on the balcony of his cabin? Margie wasn't sure what to say and felt a bit flustered. George sensed her hesitancy and reassured her it didn't really matter to him where they were as long as they were together. Margie did a mental check of whether she had sexy underwear on or not and then blushed at what she had just thought. She was glad the lighting was dim where they were sitting.

After a moment she agreed that it would be nice to sit on the balcony, which was a bit more sheltered than the open deck, and so George escorted her to his cabin. Well, it was more of a suite really and not nearly as cramped as 12b with its two single beds. It was absolutely beautiful and took Margie's breath away.

While George was opening a bottle of champagne from the bar in his room, her doubt meter went into overdrive.

How much do I know about this man? Am I safe with him? What about if he gets hot and heavy? Is there a panic button in this room or do I just shout for help over the balcony?

George crossed the room and handed her a glass of champagne and gently kissed her cheek. "Let's toast," he said. "To being lucky enough at our time of life to meet someone with whom we feel comfortable and want to see more of." Margie was thrilled but wasn't quite sure what the "want to see more of" entailed. Did he mean spend more time with her as she was or her with fewer clothes on? She was in a quandary, but he just took her by the hand and guided her through the doors onto the balcony. The sky was inky black with a million stars, and George took her in his arms and kissed her in a very satisfactory way. Margie's heart soared, and she kissed him right back, in a very satisfactory way.

He asked her if she wanted to stay the night with him, but she was still unsure about what she wanted from this relationship—if that was what it was. She knew she wanted him to be more than a friend but how much more was still undecided. She answered him honestly and said that she wasn't ready for that level of intimacy just yet, that she liked him a lot and enjoyed his company immensely. George, being the gentleman he was, although disappointed, reassured her that he understood perfectly, and he would walk her back to her cabin whenever she wanted to go. She left his cabin at two and realised it was probably the latest hour she had ever been out with a man and felt deliciously decadent.

The last full day on board arrived and there was to be a farewell ball in the evening. Fortunately Margie had packed a really beautiful cocktail dress, chosen by the girls, and at the time it had seemed hideously expensive. However, when her hair was done and make-up complete, she slid the dress down over her body and was stunned at her reflection. She had never looked so glamorous in her whole life and was thrilled to bits.

She had arranged to meet George for a drink in their favourite cocktail bar before dinner, and when she walked in the look on his face told her everything she needed to know. She felt so confident and self-assured and would make sure she thanked the girls profusely when she got home for making her spend money on this electric blue creation she was wearing. Her silver sandals just peeped out from the hem of her dress and long slim pendant earrings graced her ears with a matching bracelet encircling her wrist. She felt fabulous—and she looked stunning.

George walked across the room with his arms wide open and wrapped them gently around Margie, then giving her a kiss on the cheek. She felt so happy with this lovely man and hoped that when they were back on dry land they would see each other again and again.

The crew had done a marvellous job decorating the showroom with balloons and the tables looked spectacular with flowers and candles. It was so romantic, and Margie and George were both thrilled to be with each other. He put his arm around her waist and said, "Let's go and enjoy our last shipboard dinner together, but I hope we can have many more meals once we are on home turf." She smiled up at him and nodded her approval of these sentiments.

When dinner was over the orchestra tuned up and the dancing began. Margie and George fit together like a hand and a glove and glided around the floor as though they had been dancing together for years. Little thoughts kept popping into her head about this being a shipboard romance that wouldn't last back in the real world, but then another thought would take over—she had never been happier. She admonished herself that she should just live in the moment, because it was a long time since she had felt like she did on farewell night.

The evening came to a close at one, and George walked Margie to the door of cabin 12b. Rebecca was nowhere to be found, but Margie correctly guessed she was with Alexander having their own private farewell night celebration. George put his arms around Margie and gently kissed her on the mouth and said he would see her in the morning when they disembarked. They arranged a time to meet at the terminal once their luggage had been retrieved and Margie reluctantly said good night.

Rebecca arrived back in the cabin about a half hour later and regaled Margie with all her evening's activities. "Will you see Alexander again?"

Rebecca threw back her head and just laughed. "Not likely, he has an ex-wife and three children back home and lives in a different state.

It was just a shipboard romance, nothing more, and I have had a great time with him, but it is back to the real world tomorrow."

"What about you, Margie? You seem very taken with George. Do you think you will see him when we leave this floating magical world?"

Margie replied that she certainly hoped so and George had intimated that he would like to see her again too. "We will see what happens, but I hope we do keep seeing each other, Rebecca. I really like him, and he is so nice to me."

Chapter 35

The next morning the two women were a bit the worse for wear after a late night and probably a few too many glasses of champagne. They managed to make it to breakfast before the tables were cleared and then set about packing their bags for disembarking. They were just throwing things in their suitcases because they really should have packed the night before.

"I hope we haven't left anything behind," Margie said just as they were hauling their hand luggage along the corridor. They were almost ready to leave the ship when she remembered she had left her shoes from last night somewhere in the room. "I will only be a minute," she reassured Rebecca, "and if you see George would you tell him I will be off the ship soon?"

Rebecca nodded and just kept heading for the gangway as Margie turned back for their cabin, which proved a bit more time consuming than she'd calculated as she was going against the tide of guests leaving the ship. She finally reached cabin 12b, found her shoes, and once again made for the exit.

She had a glimpse of the terminal on the way through and was mortified when she saw George with his arms around another woman.

Margie couldn't believe her eyes and wasn't sure that she wanted this two-timer in her life anymore. He had told her he was a widower, but perhaps he'd had a lapse of memory about being single. It wouldn't be the first time a man had forgotten he was married!

With tears in her eyes Margie finally caught up with Rebecca and when her friend saw the state she was in she was horrified. "What ever is the matter, Margie? You look like you have seen a ghost and you are shaking all over."

Margie managed, between sobs and hiccups, to convey that she had seen George being greeted by another woman.

Rebecca couldn't speak for a moment but finally got out, "Where is he? I will tear him limb from limb for upsetting you."

Margie pointed in the general direction she had seen George and the "other woman" and Rebecca took off, teetering on her high heels, before Margie could restrain her. It didn't take her long to locate George, who was standing with his arm around the shoulders of the other woman. Rebecca went up to him and yelled in his face "What do you think you are doing? You have upset my best friend, and she is inconsolable. If you already have someone in your life, the decent thing would have been to tell her, not promise her the world and then whip it away from under her feet." George finally managed to get a word in and when he did it brought Rebecca's angry tirade to an instant full stop. "This is my sister, Angie. We share a villa as we are both by ourselves."

Rebecca stammered, "Oh, sorry. I thought you were two-timing my friend, and I wasn't having you hurt her. She is one of the world's lovely people."

George had a bemused expression on his face. "Yes, Rebecca, I completely agree with you, and now we should go and find Margie before she decides I am not worth looking for. That would break my heart you know because I really love that friend of yours, and I want to be with her for as much time as we have left."

Just then Rebecca waved her hand and beckoned Margie over. In the five minutes that Rebecca had been searching for George and then berating him for his treatment of her best friend, Margie had been able to repair some of the ravages of tear-stained makeup and looked reasonably presentable.

"Hello, Margie, come and meet my sister Angie. We share a villa because we are both widowed and it seemed a sensible solution to ward off loneliness," George explained. "I was telling Angie all about you when Rebecca appeared and started yelling at me for two-timing you, which I would never do."

Rebecca had the grace to look apologetic, but George reassured her that Margie was lucky to have such a great friend, and Rebecca replied, "She was very kind to me years ago, and I have never forgotten that. I am just grateful that we have found each other again and hope we stay friends forever."

Bags were collected, and George asked Margie what she would like to do and she replied, "Rebecca and I will go back to our hotel first, I will freshen up and meet you for dinner later. Is that okay with you?"

He gave her a wonderful smile, kissed her softly on the lips, and said, "It is more than okay and just as last night was farewell, tonight will be welcome, hopefully to the rest of our days together."

--o0o--

Chapter 36

Caromar Cookies had become more than just a job to all of them. Caroline's confidence had soared under Margie's gentle umbrella of love. Lindy had found a new purpose to her life and loved the interaction with the customers as they came and went each day. She knew most of them by name and had a remarkable memory for the minutiae of their life. She often enquired about their husband, children, or new job, and the customers felt they really mattered to this lovely woman who ran their favourite coffee shop.

At their second dinner meeting (the first one being taken up with hilarious anecdotes of her time on the ship) Margie wanted to know what the girls had planned for the next five years of the business as Lindy had come back on board, and they could now move forward.

Caroline outlined expansion plans for the baking and distribution of cookies, but they needed to know what Amanda had in mind for marketing. As Caroline pointed out, it was not much good baking cookies and not being able to get them out in the marketplace.

It was obvious that they were lucky to have the perfect person, Amanda, to oversee their marketing. They suggested that they would pay her a wage if she could organise what was required to start marketing their cookies on a greater scale. With Amanda's business background she had been in contact with many people and knew just where to go for help and advice. She could work from home, be there for Jamie after school, and be free to attend any events. It was the perfect fit, and Amanda was delighted. She was a hard worker and was determined that she wouldn't let them down.

Brian had turned out to be the best organiser of deliveries that Amanda had ever seen, and their customer base was expanding by the week. They had all found their niche in this expanding company that started off by a divorced woman needing to rebuild her life and a young mother who desired marital freedom above all else, baking cookies from her mother's recipes.

A week later when all the excitement had died down a little, Margie asked the girls to come to her home for a "CH & CH Night." They all looked bewildered, and Lindy asked, "Does that stand for Cha Cha?" and they all laughed. Margie explained that it was a Cheese and Champers night, because she had had another idea and wanted to run it past them. They were curious and tried to find out what she wanted to tell them, but Margie just said, "All will be revealed at seven tonight".

The girls arrived at Margie's, on time, Caroline with Gavin and Amanda with Jamie, and settled them down with a DVD. It was past their bedtime, but the children would go to sleep when they were ready. Margie had already made arrangements for the children to stay the night, as it was Friday so no school tomorrow. She also loved having the children to herself for a few hours, and they all got along famously.

When everyone was settled with a drink Margie outlined her plan. She told the girls that she really only wanted a role in the business whereby she could come and go as cruises or flights to exotic locations dictated. She also now had George in her life and he was becoming a very important part of it. She still wanted to have an income from the business, so she proposed that the three girls be quarter-share partners with her having the fourth share.

They all just looked at her in amazement and then, almost as one voice, they asked, "But how will we pay for it?"

Margie then dropped her own private bombshell. "You don't have to. It is my gift to you as I love you all so much and you have given me a life I never thought I would have—children, oh, and grandchildren too." Each of the girls was stunned by the proposal but by the look of joy on Margie's face, they couldn't help but feel that they were indeed a family.

--oOo--

CPSIA information can be obtained at www.ICGtesting.com
Printed in the USA
LVOW11*1318130616

492384LV00004B/8/P